Ken Cotterill has been a football fan and player ever since he received a football book for Christmas when he was eight. He has written over twenty plays, several short stories and two novels. Apart from football, he likes boxing, history, politics, geography and theatre. He writes an arts column for his local newspaper and directs plays. He has been an insurance collector, a wharf labourer, a storeman, a soldier in the Australian Army and a librarian. Ken supports Sheffield United and Plymouth Argyle. He has two sons and lives in Far North Queensland with his wife, Marlene.

Ken Cotterill can be contacted at
grapeguy@qld.chariot.net.au

Thank you, Mary Green, for guiding me to Tickhill.

Ken Cotterill

WHEN SATURDAY NEVER COMES

A Football Fable

AUSTIN MACAULEY PUBLISHERS™

LONDON • CAMBRIDGE • NEW YORK • SHARJAH

A CIP catalogue record for this title is available from the British Library.

ISBN 9781528995108 (Paperback)
ISBN 9781528995115 (ePub e-book)

www.austinmacauley.com

First Published 2022
Austin Macauley Publishers Ltd®
1 Canada Square
Canary Wharf
London
E14 5AA

Prologue

Three o'clock on a Saturday afternoon was a magic time for English football supporters. That was the time that supporters looked forward to all week. The occasion when they and thousands of others would stand or sit in unity to support their club. It didn't matter which club they supported. It was their club, the one they felt part of, the one that was a big part of their life. Now all that was gone.

Football in England had undergone dramatic changes over the last few years. The four major divisions had been dissolved. All ninety-two league clubs had been disbanded. Even the lower leagues had been dissolved. Park football and schoolboy teams had also been banned. Even football on patches of grass and in backyards had been banned. Football had changed drastically.

There is only one official football league in England now. That is the English Super League comprising of only four clubs. These clubs are Merseyside FC, Manchester Unity FC, Birmingham Villa FC and London City FC. By state law, no other football club can exist. No one can play football apart from the players who play for these clubs. Football in England is now all about the 'big four'.

The four clubs are immensely rich. They are run by mega-rich owners who think nothing of splashing out millions on players for their respective teams. Each club plays in a modern stadium and they each have a massive worldwide fan base. Because of this global audience, kick-off times have changed. Instead of the traditional Saturday afternoon kick-off, the games, played exclusively between the four teams, now kick off at 1.30 am on Tuesday mornings.

Saturday just doesn't matter anymore.

Life in the Royal Oak, Tickhill, South Yorkshire

It was a cold, grey November afternoon. A Saturday afternoon. The Royal Oak public house in Tickhill was doing reasonable business. Some lads were playing snooker, others chucking darts at a well-worn board. Others were huddled in warm corners drinking. After all, where do out of work football supporters go on Saturday afternoons?

Billy Glossop, wrapped in his thick coat, sat in the usual corner, staring at his phone and nursing his pint glass. Opposite sat his long-time mate, Spud Dickson. Spud, also wrapped in a thick coat, was eating crisps. Beside Spud sat Amanda Harper, Spud's sometime girlfriend. Amanda, tall, blonde and cute, was also drinking from a pint glass. Nobody spoke. They were waiting. Waiting for Trevor Wilson.

Billy, an unemployed gardener, had been in a semi-unconscious state for some time now. His beloved Rotherham United had long since gone. The club's New York Stadium had been bulldozed and turned into a fertiliser factory. Life as he knew it had ended the day the Millers had ceased to exist. Billy still followed football. He had a mild interest in the distant Mongolian-Gobi Desert Premier League, in which he half-heartedly supported Ulan Bator Rangers. But it was no substitute for his beloved Rotherham United.

Spud, an unemployed van driver, was the same. His handsome features were often creased with hidden pain. He claimed to have committed suicide twice after his beloved Scunthorpe United had been dissolved. But somehow, he remained among the living, determined to one day see his team rise from the ashes. But it was a day he knew would probably never come. Spud, like Billy, was a half-hearted fan of a distant league; the Tibetan Hillside League, in which he half-heartedly supported Mount Everest Town. But it was no substitute for his beloved Scunthorpe United.

Both Billy and Spud had tried to take interest in other sports, but the team names, such as Bulls, Titans, Eagles, Hornets, Sharks, Dolphins and Cats had them totally confused.

"Who the bloody hell is who?" said Billy.

"What game are they playing?" said Spud.

For Billy and Spud, the only game was football.

As for Amanda, she had pretended to be a Scunthorpe United fan to please Spud, but in reality, she had followed Scunthorpe United's main rival Grimsby Town, a club whose ground and training facilities had recently been turned into a lime pit. But she loved Spud, or at least she thought she did. And what bothered Spud bothered Amanda. For now. Then Trevor arrived.

Trevor Turns Up

He walked into the Royal Oak, donkey coat firmly buttoned, bringing a cold draught from outside with him. He plonked himself into a vacant seat next to Billy and grunted a greeting. Spud buried himself even further into his heavy coat. Billy gave Trevor a nod. Amanda ignored him.

Surprisingly, Trevor, an unemployed revolutionary, was the one who still had some energy. Trevor had been a fanatical Doncaster Rovers fan before the 'Great Disruption' as the dissolution of the Football League was dubbed by the tabloid press. But somehow, he seemed to have some life in him. Spud suspected that Trevor was a secret Birmingham Villa FC fan on account of Trevor having a great aunt who lived near Coventry. Spud thought that the 'Great Disruption' hadn't upset Trevor at all. They had had strong words, but nothing had been proved.

"Right, what's the go?" said Trevor, rubbing his hands.

"Nothing's the go, Trev, unless you mean whose funeral is it?" said Amanda.

Nobody laughed. Spud finished the crisps.

"Why are you so happy then, eh?" said Billy, glancing at Trevor.

"Me? Happy? After what they have done to my Doncaster Rovers?" said Trevor.

Doncaster Rovers' ground had been recently bulldozed and was now being transformed into a chicken farm. The redevelopment progress by Ukrainian bulldozer drivers had been shown on the daily television news program, *Look North and No Further* only last week.

"Come on, you look happy, tell us?" said Amanda.

Trevor liked Amanda but for some reason, he felt she didn't like him.

"All right. Get me a pint and I'll tell you," said Trevor, looking at Billy.

Billy looked at Spud then reluctantly got up and went over to the bar. Billy moved so slowly you would have sworn he had cement slabs in his pockets. He returned with a pint for Trevor and a couple of bags of crisps for the group. Amanda opened the crisps and tucked in.

"So, what's up?" said Spud.

"Yeah, what's up?" said Amanda.

Trevor indicated for them to come closer. Reluctantly, Billy, Spud and Amanda leaned over the pub table. Trevor kept them in suspense for a few more seconds before speaking.

"I've had an idea," said Trevor.

"That's good," said Amanda, "nobody has ever had an idea before."

Undeterred, Trevor ploughed on.

"Listen. We form a resistance group."

"A resistance group? Resistance to what, eh?" said Billy.

Trevor shook his head. Beneath his coat and woolly jumper, he was wearing his red Karl Marx T-shirt. He felt empowered.

"Have you been asleep this past year or so? The Great Disruption. That's what. Football as we know it, gone. We form a resistance group and fight to win our club's back so that football will be like it used to be. Remember? So that we will be on the terraces on Saturday afternoons supporting our wonderful teams and not here, drinking crap beer, scoffing soggy crisps and looking like death warmed up."

Trevor had been planning that little speech for weeks. Nobody spoke. Encouraged, he continued.

"We take back what is ours, our clubs. The proletariat fight back! We get rid of the mega-clubs, the mega-rich owners. We get rid of that mad American bastard who is running this crap. We get rid of the capitalist scum who have ruined our lives! We fight for football as it used to be. Four divisions and kick-offs on Saturday at 3 pm! That's what we do!"

Amanda reached for a crisp and yawned.

"How do we do that, then?" said Amanda.

"Yeah, yeah, how?" echoed Spud.

"We fight!" said Trevor, waving a fist.

Trevor had recently watched a documentary on the French student and workers' strikes of 1968. Everybody in the film seemed to be waving their fists.

"What with?" said Billy, "the mega-clubs have got all the money, they have the politicians in their pocket, eh. Especially that American ratbag. They have power. They have the Anti-Football Police on their side. What can we do? The Scots tried it and look what happened to them, eh."

"Yeah, look what happened to them," said Amanda, knowingly.

Billy was referring to fans in Scotland resisting the Scottish version of the 'Great Disruption.' There the game had been banned totally. Scots in all the major cities had come out into the streets in large numbers, demonstrating for the return of their clubs.

Thousands of Celtic and Rangers fans, united for the first time ever, as well as all six supporters from Arbroath, all five from Montrose and three from Peterhead, had taken to the streets of Glasgow one April morning. This had ended in disaster as thousands had been clubbed, beaten and arrested by the black-uniformed Anti-Football Police and then deported to the Faroe Islands.

Many were still there, living in bleak football detention centres on windswept clifftops, reduced to collecting bird's eggs to survive. Several had escaped and were wanted fugitives. Many political football prisoners were still in hiding in the Orkneys, the Shetlands and other remote, wave-battered islands. Life for true football believers in Scotland was appalling, scary and very dangerous.

"I'm not going to be sent to the Faroe Islands, yeah," said Spud.

"Me neither, eh," said Billy, shivering at the thought.

Neither of them knew where the Faroe Islands were, but they knew it was an awful place.

"Nobody is going to be sent to the bloody Faroe Islands or anywhere else," said Trevor.

Trevor was determined that his great idea would not be shot down at the first hurdle.

"So, what kind of resistance are you proposing, then?" said Amanda.

14

Trevor took a sip of his pint and grimaced. Revolution was not an easy game.

"Listen, we don't do any of that demo crap what the Scots did. Right? Nobody is going to get arrested or get their skull cracked open. My plan is much more sophisticated than that."

"Oh, yeah?" said Billy, suddenly seeing himself collecting gulls' eggs on a steep, wind-blasted cliff face and being forced to strike up an incomprehensible conversation with a Stenhousemuir supporter.

"Sophisticated? Sounds good. So, what is it then, this plan?" said Amanda.

Trevor looked around the bar before speaking, his face a mask of determination. The four friends, who were roughly about the same age, leaned over the pub table.

"Right. Tuck in a little closer and I'll tell you."

The House of Commons, Westminster

The English Super League was governed by the members of the House of Commons after the Football Association, the Premier League and the Football League had dissolved themselves following inducements from the four owners of the mega clubs. The mega-owners felt it would be easier to control a group of politicians than it would to control boards made up of members who had some integrity and a moral compass.

The Prime Minister, Tony Campbell, his greying hair beautifully coiffed, was an avid English Super League fan. He was a close friend of the owners, especially the most powerful of the mega-club owners, Hank Sharkey. In gratitude for his co-operation in having normal football abolished, Sharkey had allowed Campbell's private company, Guttersnipe Holdings (based in Panama), to have the world-wide franchise on ESL kits and supporter accessories. Campbell also had free use of Sharkey's luxury yacht and beachside mansion in Barbados.

Tonight, the House of Commons was about to vote on a bill that pertained to the English Super League. All other legislation, like an increase in the number of nurses, the old-age pensioners winter fuel allowance and help for the poor and housing assistance had been cast aside for a far more important piece of legislation.

The bill had been debated, but its passage was assured. The betting was that all 650 members of the House of Commons would vote to pass the *English Super League Rules Amendment Bill.* Parliamentary members of the British Conservative Labour Liberal Party waited patiently for the Speaker of the House to ask them for their vote.

The crux of the bill contained demands by Hank Sharkey. Sharkey wanted the game of soccer 'livened up' as he called it. To Sharkey, soccer was a bore, a great money earner, but a total bore. Sharkey wanted more action on the field and he was determined to have it.

In this legislation, Sharkey wanted offside abolished, a secret, masked twelfth player to be on one of the teams, penalties to be allowed anytime in the game irrespective of fouls in the penalty area, players sent off and then allowed back on again and supplementary goals allowed by the referee at his discretion at any time in the game. Sharkey was also strongly in favour of cardboard referees, half a goal being awarded, wrestling and a clown performing on the pitch during a game.

Sharkey believed that these changes to the rules would make the game much more exciting to watch, especially for American fans.

By late evening the bill passed the House, 649 to 1. The only objection came from Peter (Lonely) Corbett the member for Tickhill.

New York, New York

While Trevor was informing his mates of his plan, Hank Sharkey, owner of London City FC, was settling down into a soft leather chair in the sumptuous boardroom of his New York penthouse office overlooking Central Park. Sharkey was in a good mood. Boy, was he in a good mood? Two days ago, he had sold every unit in his new hotel complex in the Cayman Islands even before the complex was built. Sharkey had netted a cool 40 million dollars almost overnight. Now the sixty-five-year-old billionaire was excited about his latest plan; a plan he would reveal to his special guests who were due in the boardroom anytime soon. Hank Sharkey did not have to wait long.

The first guest to arrive was Lord Milford. Milford had a permanent tan, white teeth and jet-black hair. Although he was in his seventies, he looked only sixty-nine-years old. Milford was from old money; his ancestors having been part of Henry Tudor's mercenary army way back in August 1485. His only hobby was making money. He just loved money.

Next to arrive was Boris Igoravitch, an East European oligarch and the owner of Birmingham Villa FC. Boris, who had just jetted in from Yakadakastan, had made his money out of selling tins of baked beans on the black market. He was fifty-five years old, bald, fat and obscenely wealthy. Boris always travelled with his well-armed ten-man entourage and five gorgeous Yakadak escorts. Boris always carried a small tin of baked beans in his inside pocket just in case.

Finally, Jose Sanchez walked through the door. Tall and lean and the youngest of the group at forty-eight, Sanchez was the owner of Merseyside FC. Despite his Spanish sounding name, he was Icelandic. But although he was Icelandic, he spoke English in a fractured Spanish accent. He had made his money from gambling, mainly from predicting which Icelandic volcano would erupt next. Like the others, he was mega-rich, but wanted more, much more.

The four multi-billionaires had first assembled in a high-class London hotel a few years ago. Each was interested in causing a disease that they could profit from by 'inventing' a cure. They had got on well that night in London. After the meeting, they had each selected an attractive looking waitress and retired to their respective hotel rooms. Some years later, realising the large amounts of money to be made from football, they had met again and decided to create the now-famous English Super League. So far, things had gone well.

"Gentlemen, welcome, welcome," said Sharkey, standing and shaking their respective hands.

"So, what is this all about, my dear chap?" said Lord Milford.

"Yeah. What is all about, uh?" grunted Boris.

"Amigos, I have little time, I have bullfight to attend in Reykjavik this afternoon," said Jose, looking admiringly at the tallest of the Yakadak escorts.

"Patience, gentlemen, I'll get to the point of this meeting all in due time. Now, please, sit down," said Sharkey, gesturing to the empty chairs tucked in close to the big boardroom table.

The guests, the escorts and Boris's bodyguards did Sharkey's bidding and eased themselves into seats at the boardroom table. All looked eagerly at Sharkey. Sharkey smiled and seated himself in his leather power chair. In front of each businessman was a drinking glass and a jug of water filled to the brim with New York's finest tap water.

One of the escorts pulled out a nail file and began working away at her long nails. Another applied a second coat of lipstick, while another combed her thick, black hair. Sharkey was momentarily distracted before turning on the charm for his guests.

"Gentlemen, it's good of you to make it at such short notice. First, I have some good news. As we speak, the new rules we talked about last time we met will have been passed in that dumb fossil house called the House of Commons. From my point of view and that of the American public, I have witnessed two seasons of utter boredom. I assure you gentlemen, these changes to the rules will make soccer much more exciting to watch."

Sharkey had gone through the new rules with the other owners some weeks ago. Lord Milford and Jose Sanchez had been highly dubious at first. But after a sizable donation to their respective bank accounts they fully agreed with the changes.

"Now, there is more. What I have to tell you has only one objective and one objective only, and that is to make all of you and myself, money. Lots of money."

Boris, Jose and Lord Milford leaned forward in their respective seats.

Lord Milford briefly looked at the others before nominating himself as the spokesman for the group.

"Do go ahead and tell us, old chap, we are all ears."

Sharkey smiled, then revealed his plan.

Trevor Outlines His Plan Again

"Could you just go through that again? I didn't get half of it," said Billy.

"Me and all," said Spud, scratching his head.

Trevor gave a mock sigh.

"Yeah, all right, no problem," said Trevor.

Trevor didn't mind having to repeat what he had just said because he noticed that Amanda had gone quiet. She had moved away from Spud and inched a bit closer to him.

"Let me go through it again," said Trevor, glancing at Amanda.

"Yeah, you go through it again," said Amanda.

"Right, here we go again. First, where did the owners of the super league clubs get their cash? That is important for what I have in mind. Now, Hank Sharkey is the owner of London City FC. He's the American who started all this super league bullshit. He's the richest and most powerful of them all. But, he's a total fruitcake."

"I'd love to get me hands on him, eh," said Billy.

"To continue. He got his money from his grandfather on his dad's side. The grandfather got the money from marrying a Red Indian squaw in Oklahoma."

"What, a real Red Indian as in the cowboy films?" said Spud.

"She was rich this squaw, then?" said Billy.

"The tribe were. Now this tribe in Oklahoma, the Osage tribe, had been put on crap land, but underneath was oil, lots of it. The tribe was sitting on richest vein of oil in the whole of Oklahoma. So, poor white guys with eyes on the oil money married squaws and then killed them. It was a big case at the time. Back in the 1920s. The FBI and J. Edgar Hoover and all that stuff."

"Didn't a Hoover once play for Rochdale?" said Spud.

Amanda elbowed Spud in the ribs.

"How do you know this?" said Amanda, with a slight touch of admiration in her voice.

"Because I do. Since that stupid employment act was passed last year, I spend most of my time reading in the library," said Trevor.

Trevor was referring to the *Employment Only for the Elite Act* which had been passed at the end of last year. The best jobs had only been allocated to the wealthy, former public schoolboys, people who talked posh and those that donated to Britain's one big mega-party, the British Conservative Labour Liberal Party. The crap jobs were for everybody else. Trevor, Spud, Billy and Amanda didn't even qualify for them.

"Anyway, that's just how he got his money. The scumbag. Next is Lord Milford. In case you've forgotten, he owns Manchester Unity FC. Well, he got his money from his ancestors as well. Some scumbag called Pierre de Milford came over from France in 1485 with Henry Tudor to help defeat Richard III at the Battle of Bosworth Field. When Tudor took the throne as Henry VII, he handed out chunks of land to those who had helped him," said Trevor.

"Wow, he is clever," said Amanda.

"I thought Bosworth Field was Carlisle United's home ground?" said Spud.

"Brunton Park is Carlisle's ground, Spud. Well, it was. It's a rubbish dump now," said Billy.

"Continuing. Huge chunks of land were given to this Pierre de Milford by a grateful Henry Tudor, which the current Lord Milford inherited. When they built the new M777 and the new rail link to Scotland, Milford sold chunks of his land to the government for a fortune. Went into the billions. Taxpayers' money was given to the bastard."

"I've been on the M777. It's massive. Ten lanes both sides," said Amanda.

"That's for a reason, Amanda. Milford stipulated the M777 to be that wide so they would have to pay him more money for the land they bought from him. He stole from us, us taxpayers."

"The robbing scum. Taking my hard-earned taxes," said Spud.

"Hark at him. You haven't worked for the last two years, Spud. What taxes have you paid?" said Amanda.

Spud took a swig of his beer.

"I'd love to get me hands on him an all, eh." said Billy.

"Milford's ancestors were also involved in the slave trade in the West Indies and Central America. Jamaica, British Honduras. When Britain abolished slavery these scum bastards received compensation for losing their slaves. The rich-looking after the rich. Sort of a welfare state for the wealthy only. Do you know that current taxpayers have only just finished paying off that loan?"

"I didn't know that," said Amanda.

Trevor took a quick swig of his beer before continuing. Things were going well.

"Right, next is Boris Igoravitch from Yakadakistan. He owns Birmingham Villa FC. He owes his billions to his brother, Vladimir, who came to power in a bloody coup a few years back. Vladimir is a right head case. A total nut job. Vladimir killed thousands of innocent people, looted the state bank and then gave Boris the only profitable factories in the country. The baked bean factories."

"I've never eaten baked beans since," said Spud.

"Then we have Jose Sanchez, the Icelander with the fake Spanish accent. He owns Merseyside FC. His ancestors were soldiers on the Spanish Armada, way back in 1580s or something. Their ship went around the top of Scotland and got blown by a storm out to Iceland. Sanchez's ancestor was the sole survivor. He got picked up by some Icelanders in a small boat. Apparently, after that, he never left Iceland. Fast forward a few centuries to Jose. He got into banking. Rumour is he stole all the money from the banks in Iceland before the crash in 2008. He now runs an online betting business, which among other things takes bets on which volcano will erupt next in Iceland."

"I'd like to stuff him in a volcano," said Billy.

"The point of me mentioning where these capitalist scumbags got their money from is so that we won't feel guilty when we take it from them. Without their money, there will be no so-called super clubs in a bloody four-team super league."

"Yeah, too right. But how are we going to take their money, eh?" said Billy.

"Well pay attention this time and I'll explain it again," said Trevor, winking at Amanda.

Film Time

"OK gentlemen, this is my plan. It's about robotics. Yes, robotics. Now, let me show you how Robotic Projected Recordings actually works," said Sharkey, confident his plan was foolproof.

Magically, three gofers entered the boardroom and quickly set up a giant panoramic screen, a screen that blocked everyone's view of Central Park.

"Right, gentlemen, just pay attention to what I am about to show you."

All eyes turned to the screen. On the screen, a London City FC player, Silvio Battersby, appeared. It was an interview concerning his well-publicised tantrum last month on why he was only being paid one million pounds a week when he believed he should be paid much more. Battersby had mansions and villas scattered around the world and at least fifteen luxury cars. He also had a body deodorant and a drain cleaning fluid named after himself.

"Just listen to the greedy bastard. You know, he also wanted a butler, a toothpaste allowance, a bootlace allowance, a facial cream allowance, a body odour allowance and a new tattoo allowance," said Sharkey.

"He, greedy son-of-a bitch," grumbled Boris.

"Yes, a terribly greedy man," said Lord Milford.

"He needs teaching a lesson," said Jose, playing with his replica gold colt revolver.

"Well, with Robotic Projected Recordings, we will teach him a lesson and then we won't need to worry anymore about the Silvio Battersbys of this world," said Sharkey, with a chuckle.

Lord Milford edged his chair closer to the table.

"How do you mean, old chap?" said Lord Milford.

"How do I mean? You English. How you ever had an empire I'll never know. Listen. We got rid of football agents, right? We got rid of egotistical coaches, right? It's time now for phase three. We now get rid of Battersby and all the rest of the players at our respective clubs."

There was a pause as Sharkey's words sank in.

"Get rid of the players, old chap?"

"As in kill them?" said Boris, enthusiastically.

"Exactly. We get rid of them. The players. Every one of the whinging, whining bastards."

There was a pause for a few seconds.

"But, Hank, how will we have a super league if we get rid of all the players? After all it's a cash cow, dear boy."

Sharkey leaned back in his chair and laughed at Lord Milford.

"Fooled, you all. I knew I would. You see, that face on the screen is not Silvio Battersby my one million pounds a week whinging quarterback," said Sharkey.

"Centre back. He is a centre back," said Jose.

"Whatever."

"Then who is it?" said Lord Milford, puzzled.

"Who is it? You mean what is it? I'll tell you. It's a robot. A robot that looks, talks and plays like a real footballer. Had you fooled, uh?"

Sharkey laughed. Everybody in the room looked impressed, even the escorts.

"Now let me show you this," said Sharkey, beaming, as he pressed a button on the remote control.

The screen was now showing a game of football. Players in red and players in blue. It looked like last month's game between Manchester Unity FC and Birmingham Villa FC.

"Now, I bet all of you think that what you are seeing right now is a real soccer game, right?"

Everybody nodded. It certainly looked real enough. Hank laughed again.

"Now, let me tell you something. Every player in that clip is a robot, a robot made to look like the real deal. The real player. They run, they tackle, they shoot, they pass, they sweat, they swear, they move from offence to defence, just like the real human players do in real soccer games. They even have the same hairstyle and the same stupid tattoos. Except, except gentlemen, they are all robots. Beautifully engineered robots."

Again, everybody was impressed.

"So, are you saying, that these robots will replace real human players?" said Lord Milford.

"That's right, Lord Baby. What a genius you are. There will be no more moaning players wanting more and more money. What we do, gentlemen, is we replace them with look-a-like robots who will cost us nothing. I repeat, they will cost us nothing. Now, am I a genius or am I not?" said Sharkey, glaring at his guests.

Capitalist Running Dogs

Back in the Royal Oak, Trevor was getting excited explaining his plan.

"We get on the dark web and remove the capitalist running-dogs of their money," said Trevor, his head bobbing in agreement to his own words.

He had read the words 'capitalist running-dogs' in some old Maoist literature he had picked up at a second-hand bookshop. He thought the words would make him sound like a cool, well-read revolutionary.

"We log in, work out their passwords and transfer the money to..." Trevor suddenly hesitated.

Amanda sighed. She had heard mad ideas before, but this one sounded insane and she said so.

"Transfer the money to where, oh 'capitalist running-dog?' Are you saying that if we log on to this dark web we can find out where these ratbags have stashed their money and then we just press some numbers on a keyboard and steal it?"

Trevor nodded lamely. Suddenly he didn't feel in control anymore.

"Look, if cyber theft was that easy it would have been done by now. Their money will be protected by firewalls behind firewalls that no one will be able to crack," said Amanda.

"Cybermen. Seen them in Dr Who episodes," said Spud, smiling.

Amanda gave Spud a hefty nudge with her elbow. Trevor paused to nervously slurp his pint glass dry.

"Look, experienced trolls would have raided the dark web sites ages ago, found where the money is and lifted it," said Amanda.

Trevor's heart sank, but he pretended to look unconcerned.

"Dark web. Isn't that full of dark satanic stuff?" said Spud.

"No, you goose. It's just web sites that can't be reached by normal internet providers. The sites are normally a bit iffy. Secretive and illicit. Selling drugs or money laundering, that kind of stuff," explained Amanda.

"Listen, I think I know which bank they all bank with," said Trevor, trying to regain the initiative.

"What, the one on the corner of the High Street?" said Billy, laughing.

"No. The Global World Bank is the bank I think they all bank with," said Trevor.

"Not the Yorkshire Penny Bank, then?" said Spud.

Billy laughed again. Amanda shook her head.

"Look, these guys don't bank with normal banks or building societies like we do. Get real. Come on. They rob banks. Look at Sanchez and what he did with the Icelandic banks? All their ill-gotten gains are in banks or institutions that we have never heard of and will never hear of. Their money is in Switzerland, Lichtenstein, the Cayman Islands, Panama, the Isle of Man or some Pacific Island places that I can't remember. What I do know is that it is not in any normal bank," said Amanda.

"We had a holiday on the Isle of Man once when I was a kid. I couldn't find a toilet. I had to have a dump under a bush," said Spud.

"Oh, do be serious!" said Amanda.

Amanda felt her face flush. She had all their attention. Her words were being absorbed. Suddenly, she felt that she was no longer an appendage to Spud. Quietness descended around the pub table. Laughter could be heard from distant snooker players accompanied by the clink of snooker balls. Darts speared silently into the dartboard.

"What do we do now, then?" said Spud, looking at Amanda.

"Yeah, all right, Miss Genius, what's next?" said Trevor.

For the first time as far as she could remember, Amanda was the centre of attention. She was proud that she was a self-proclaimed fighter for downtrodden causes. After all, her late Uncle Ron had been a prominent member of the Communist Party of South Yorkshire (Trotsky Faction). Fighting for just causes was in her DNA. But as she looked at the faces of her football emaciated mates, she had no idea what to say next, no idea at all.

Death Most Diabolical

The room had been cleared of Boris's bodyguards and the glamorous escorts. Seated around the table were just the four main players; the mega-wealthy owners of the English Super League clubs.

Sharkey cleared his throat.

"Gentlemen, let me reveal the plan."

Jose Sanchez and Lord Milford looked at each other. They noticed Boris seemed relaxed.

"OK. Here is what we do to rid ourselves of our troublesome employees. Now pay close attention. Shortly, all four clubs will stage a special, one-off tournament in the Yakadakastan capital, Dakerdaker. The stadiums are first class and we'll give the tournament lots of publicity. We'll give it world-wide television and digital coverage. Advertising will be huge. Now, while they are in Yakadakastan we will replace the human players with the robot players."

Sharkey paused to let his words sink in.

"Replace human players with robot players? How do we do that, amigo?" said Jose.

"Ah. This is where Boris's brother, Vladimir comes in, right Boris?" said Sharkey.

"Right," said Boris.

"Right. Vladimir doesn't like any opposition. That's right isn't it, Boris?" said Sharkey, grinning.

"That's right. My brother is in charge of everything in People's Democratic Republic of Yakadakastan. It is easy. No opposition."

"That's right. No opposition. And you know why there is no opposition, gentlemen?"

"Do surprise us," said Lord Milford.

"There is no opposition because they are all dead. Wasted."

Nobody flinched. All eyes were on Hank Sharkey.

"Now pay close attention gentlemen. A few kilometres outside of the capital is a very large lake. Am I right in saying that, Boris?"

Boris nodded.

"Yes. A big lake full of acid. My brother is proud of it. It looks so beautiful at sunset," said Boris, smiling.

"Yeah, a big beautiful acid pit of a lake. And that, gentlemen, is where we dispose of our troublesome employees," said Sharkey.

"What? Drop them in the acid pit?" said Lord Milford.

"That's right, Lord Baby. We drop them in the acid pit."

Lord Milford looked at Jose.

"Every player and the reserves, too?" said Jose, wide-eyed.

"You got it, Jose. Every goddamn player and the reserves too. Anything that is human, that breathes, that moans and groans, that kicks a ball. Plop, into the pit. All the players will be gone and all our financial problems with them. It's brilliant."

"It brilliant!" echoed Boris.

Lord Milford and Jose looked at each other. Milford was aware that Sharkey had acquired his millions from his relatives who had killed Native American squaws for oil inheritance.

Lord Milford cleared his throat.

"How do we lure them to this acid pit?" said Lord Milford.

Hank laughed.

"Tell, 'em, Boris."

Boris laughed.

"My brother has a boat. Big boat. What you call a luxury yacht. He takes all players out on the lake in a yacht. The yacht has a special hull that is acid-proof. We give everyone onboard food and drinks, even beautiful girls. You know, to take minds off things. Relax them. Then, when we get to the middle of the lake..."

"You'll love this bit," said Sharkey, chortling.

"There is a special reception room in the bottom of the boat. Big room. All luxury. Thick carpet, expensive chandeliers, beautiful big piano, dramatic spiral staircase, a well-stocked bar. All well below the waterline. Everybody is lured into the room. Relax in luxury. Girls, drinks, good music. Ship goes to the middle of the lake. At right moment, captain opens the bottom of the yacht below reception room floor and all players and others disappear into the lake. Plop. Gone. All dissolved."

"And the beauty is, it's tried and tested. Tell 'em, Boris."

"It works well. Very well. You recall the rebel leader in my country, Che' Castro Smith? Big cheese in the stupidly named Yakadakastan People's Liberation Army (Central Command). He was one big pain in the ass. How you say, knucklehead? Thought he represented the people and said he could run the country more humanely than my bloodthirsty brother. He disappeared not long after peace talks broke down on the same boat on the same tranquil lake. Ha, ha! What a coincidence. He and his stupid advisers are now all gone. All dissolved in a lake," said Boris, with great pride.

"Yes, I recall reading about Smith's sudden disappearance on the CCNN online news," said Lord Milford.

"So, now you know," said Boris.

Sharkey looked at his guests and smiled.

"So, what do you think, gentlemen? Is that a plan or is that a plan?"

Amanda's Plan

Amanda pulled her hair free from her ponytail. She always did this when she was nervous and excited. She took a deep breath and turned to Billy.

"Billy, turn on your phone to last week's game between London City FC and Merseyside FC," said Amanda.

"Why?"

"Just do it."

"Do I have to?"

"Just do it!"

"But?"

"Do it!"

Billy groaned then jabbed at his phone. Within seconds the game came on. Highlights only. The camera focussed on the crowd which was a seething frenzy of excitement. Fans, mainly young people, decked out in the team colours, either blue or red, cheered every move, even goal kicks, mid-field throw-ins and the half-time whistle.

The conspirators looked on appalled.

"Look at the mad bastards. Haven't a clue about real football, eh," said Billy.

"Dead right, we've had two years of this crap," echoed Trevor, eager to keep in Amanda's good books.

"I can't put up with another year of that drivel," said Billy.

"A pack of traitors," said Spud, looking at Billy's phone.

"Scum, the lot of them," said Billy.

Billy switched off the highlights in disgust.

"You know, I've emailed fans all over the country and none of them admits to going to see these shitty, rigged ESL games," said Billy.

"Well, somebody is going to them. Look at the crowds they get. Like I say, we've had two years of this shit!" said Trevor.

"It's all crap if you ask me, rigged bollocks." said Billy.

"It's a new generation. They don't know about real football, we ought to shoot them all!" said Trevor.

"Yeah, good idea," said Billy.

Amanda judged that she had given her mates enough time to let off steam.

"All right, all right, calm down. All of you. Nobody is shooting anybody," said Amanda.

Everybody took a deep breath.

"Now, listen. Who of you lot has heard of the Spanish flu epidemic?" said Amanda.

Blank, open-mouthed faces stared back at her.

"The what?" said Spud.

Amanda shook her head. "I thought so. Well, it happened just after World War One. Have you heard of that?"

Trevor, Spud and Billy nodded.

"Well, that's something," said Amanda.

"Me grandad were in World War One. He was shot dead before he married me grandma," said Spud.

"How could he have married your grandma if he were shot dead?" said Billy.

"What?" said Spud.

"I said, how could he have married your grandma?"

"Pay attention you two." said Amanda "Never mind that. Just listen. Here is what we do. We spread a rumour on social media that all the super league grounds are infected by a flu or disease. A flu that is so deadly that it will kill anyone going to the grounds. Kill them stone dead. Then, maybe, hopefully, nobody will go to watch the games."

Trevor knew the answer to that, but was glad that Billy got in first.

"Yeah, yeah, but the bastards don't depend on who goes into the grounds for their money anymore like old times. They get their money from satellite link-ups, global advertising, digital links and global TV rights and all that bollocks," said Billy.

Amanda nodded.

"I know, I know that. But, but the crowds in the grounds, those stupid young idiots who don't know any better, give the games an atmosphere with their banners, flags and chanting. Without the crowds yelling like lunatics every two seconds the games would look a bit flat on TV. Am I right? There would be no atmosphere. Just think. Just think what it would all look like with empty stadiums? Nobody there. Seats all empty. No cheering and chanting. Just silence. Silence. Would the scum bags be able to sell a product globally that had no supporters or atmosphere?"

Silence also descended on the quartet. Amanda looked at her companions. Spud, Billy and Trevor gave this some thought. Eventually, they looked at each other, smiled and nodded. Maybe Amanda was right. With no crowds, there would be no atmosphere and if there was no atmosphere then perhaps, just perhaps, there would be no English Super League.

LaGuardia Airport

The meeting had long finished in the New York City boardroom, but Lord Milford and Jose Sanchez got together at New York's LaGuardia airport to discuss what had been said. Both were seated in the exclusive Lear Jet Lounge sipping mineral water before boarding their respective private jets for trans-Atlantic flights. Milford loosened his old-school tie.

"What do you think of what was discussed back there?" said Lord Milford.

Jose Sanchez paused before answering.

"I am glad you ask, amigo. I am not happy with what was proposed," said Sanchez.

Milford nodded.

"Ah, so, like me, you are against mass murder?"

Sanchez shrugged.

"Mass murder? No. It is not that, amigo. No. I agree with Sharkey. The players are a pain in the ass. And they want too much money. Far too greedy. No, zap the lot of them I say. No, I just don't think we will be able to fool everybody with the robots."

Milford was taken aback, but he sipped his drink casually.

"That is precisely what I was thinking, old boy. I mean, for a start their wives and girlfriends will be the first to realise that their man is acting a little strange. A little robotic should we say? And what about when they climb into bed. Can you image?"

Sanchez laughed.

"Maybe robots perform better than players, hey amigo?"

It was Milford's turn to laugh.

"You are right, old boy. You are right. The robots might fool the public, but will they pass the wife test? I think not. Unless, unless Sharkey has a dastardly plan for the wives and girlfriends as well?"

Sanchez stopped laughing. He leaned forward in his seat and stared into Lord Milford's eyes.

"I hope not. I enjoy having sex with all the players' wives and girlfriends in my club. We have regular big orgies when players are away or training. Such wonderful times we have on my giant bed in my luxury villa in Bootle. The times we have spent there. Ah, I love them all, the blondes, the brunettes, the redheads. So beautiful. You know, all of their wives and girlfriends are madly in love with me," said Sanchez, his eyes glazing with excitement.

Lord Milford was surprised by this revelation, but tried to look cool and casual. He nodded understandingly. Milford had not had a fling with another woman since that waitress many years ago when the club owners had first met in a plush London hotel. But now that his wife, Lady Penelope, had passed away perhaps it was time to seduce all the wives and girlfriends of Manchester Unity FC players, just like Jose was doing with his club's wives and girlfriends.

The thought had no sooner entered his head than he dismissed it. He knew he would have to take a bucket load of little blue tablets before he could achieve anything between the bed sheets these days. Lord Milford's glory days in the lovemaking department were long gone.

Lord Milford snapped out of his daydream.

"Yes, yes. Look, we have these crazy rule changes coming up and now this idea. Do we trust this Sharkey chap? You know that he is quite mad."

Jose nodded.

"I know, I know he is mad. How you say, bonkers. Totally bonkers. But he knows how to make money, amigo. As long as he makes money for me, I will support him," said Jose.

"Yes, I know, but what do we do, old boy. Do we go along with this insane plan, or, or do we..."?

It was Lord Milford's turn to lean forward, pause and do some intense eye staring.

"Do we do what, amigo?" said Sanchez.

Lord Milford inclined his head, stood, and finished his drink.

"Tell you what, old boy, I'll think about it and let you know what we might do. Keep in touch, Jose, keep in touch, and do enjoy the bullfight and any future orgies."

Lord Milford winked at Sanchez.

Sanchez smiled, finished his drink and followed Lord Milford to Departures.

Amanda's Kitchen

Amanda, Spud, Billy and Trevor were seated around Amanda's kitchen table. Amanda rented a small flat in Tickhill. She lived alone and was quite happy to continue to do so despite Spud's many protestations and attempts to move in. They were all drinking steaming coffee from big mugs.

"I see they've changed the rules. The House of Commons mob. It was on telly last night. Bloody useless politicians. Some crap about awarding penalties any time, supplementary goals and players in disguise," said Trevor.

"Players wearing superhero masks, I heard," said Billy.

"Yeah, I know. Unbelievable. They've been paid to pass the changes. You'd have to be paid. Nobody in their right mind would bring in rules like that. They're insane. They take effect tomorrow night for the Merseyside FC v Manchester Unity FC clash. Should be hilarious to watch," said Spud.

"Total madness! I'm not watching it," said Trevor.

"Hey, maybe we won't have to do anything. The game will just die of shame after these rule changes," said Billy, sipping his coffee.

"Yeah, that is a thought. Let the bastards kill themselves with crap!" said Trevor.

Amanda wasn't listening.

"Look, never mind about the rule changes. We don't know the impact of them yet. Let's see what we can do. Us. So, heads together. We need a name for this flu that we're going to invent," said Amanda.

Trevor had given this lots of thought since the idea had been first broached. He had spent hours in bed at night tossing over names for the fictitious disease.

"I have a name for it. A bloody good one. We can call it the Capitalist Scum flu!" said Trevor, with pride.

"Yeah, I like that," said Billy.

"I can see it now. Write up in the paper. 'If you don't want to come down with Capitalist Scum flu don't go to any of the English Super League games ever again!' Brilliant!" said Trevor.

"What about Wanker Super League flu, eh?" said Billy.

"Yeah, Capitalist Scum Wankers flu! Brilliant!" said Trevor.

Amanda shook her head.

"Don't be daft. We can't call it that," said Amanda.

"Yeah, we can't," said Spud, nodding at Amanda.

Spud had his mind on other activity in Amanda's flat for later that night. Tonight, with her blonde hair fully down and cascading over her tight pink jumper, Amanda was all that Spud desired. For tonight at least. He just knew he had to be careful as the night wore on. If he upset her, he knew he would be home alone and not cuddled up with Amanda in her warm bed.

Trevor was not to be dissuaded.

"Why not? That's what it is, a capitalist rip-off run by a pack of wankers! Football is raw capitalism if you think about it. Look at the big clubs before the ESL was formed. All that

Premier League garbage. The so-called big six. Man U, Man City, Chelsea, Arsenal, Liverpool, Spurs. Millions upon millions of pounds spent on transfers. Millions spent on crap players from Portugal, Spain, Sardinia and Greece. Coaches with egos bigger than a blue whale. Did they give a stuff about our little teams? Did they heck. They had millions to spend and we had peanuts," said Trevor.

"And where are they now, the big six? Stuffed like Scunny and Donny!" said Spud.

"Yeah, stuffed, and I'm glad, but it's got ten times worse since. All that money that could have gone to hospitals and schools and public housing, has been wasted on bloody football! And now there are only four teams left and all the money goes to them. Four bloody teams! We have to call it Capitalist Scum flu!" said Trevor.

Billy nodded furiously.

"I know, I know, I understand what you're saying, but we can't call it that. It's too stupid. With a name like that everyone will know it's a hoax," said Amanda.

Billy looked at Trevor. There was a pause.

"Yeah, that is a possibility," said Billy, quietly.

"That's a good point, Amanda, everyone will know it's a hoax," said Spud.

"Thank you for your support, Lord Sir Echo," said Amanda, looking at Spud.

Trevor also looked at Spud but then went quiet. There was a pause as everyone took a drink from their mugs.

"Eh, this Spanish flu. How did it get its name, then?" said Billy.

"Good point, Billy. Tell us, Amanda, as you seem to be the expert on pandemics," said Trevor, with a touch of sarcasm.

Amanda leaned forward.

"Yeah, right, oh, then. It was first diagnosed in America. Kansas to be exact. American troops could have brought it to France. This was during World War One. The French censored any mention of it as it might affect morale. The war and that. But it spread into Spain as well. A member of their royal family got it. The Spanish were not at war so it was mentioned in their newspapers. Hence it became known as Spanish flu. Spain has been a bit touchy about it ever since," said Amanda.

"So, it should have really been called Yankee Bastard flu?" said Trevor.

"Or French flu?" said Billy.

"Whatever. But that's how it became known as Spanish flu. It was a real killer. Millions died. All over the world. Rich and poor," said Amanda.

"Anything that kills rich bastards is a good enough for me," said Trevor.

"Sounds like we're on to something. What can we call our epidemic, then?" said Billy.

It all went quiet around the table. Brows furrowed.

"We could name it after a country," said Spud.

"Yeah. Scotland flu or Luxembourg flu or Faroe Islands flu," said Billy.

"What about Denmark flu. I've been there, what a miserable place," said Trevor.

Amanda shook her head.

"Nah, that's too obvious. You know what, let's call it English Super League flu. ESL flu for short. That way we brand the disease with the product. So, whenever you think of the ESL you think of the killer flu as well," said Amanda.

There was another pause as Amanda's words sank in.

"I like it. Brilliant!" said Spud, eager for proceedings to be wrapped up.

"Yeah, yeah, sounds good enough to me," said Billy.

Trevor gave it some extra thought.

"Yeah, all right. I still think Capitalist Scum Wanker flu sounds better. But I'll admit Amanda has a point. Yeah, all right, I agree, we go with ESL flu," said Trevor.

Amanda smiled, then stood.

"Good. Right, well that's it then. Settled. From tonight, I want you all to get on your social outlets and spread the word. Tell the world that the ESL stadiums are infected with a killer disease. ESL flu. The symptoms are excitement and shouting wildly. That way everybody who goes to the stadiums will think they have ESL flu," said Amanda.

"Sounds crackers to me," said Trevor.

"If you have a better idea let me know, Trevor. But it's getting late and I want to go to bed. Alone," said Amanda, looking at Spud.

Everybody got the message. The lads finished their drinks and made their way slowly to Amanda's front door. They slipped their coats on and bade Amanda goodnight.

"Yeah, thanks. Same to you. See you all tomorrow in the Royal Oak," said Amanda, as she closed the door on her fellow conspirators.

Amanda watched Billy, Trevor and Spud from the kitchen window as they trooped out into the gloom and said their goodnights under the faint glow of a street light. They each then went their separate ways and disappeared from view.

As they disappeared Amanda texted one of them.

Come back if you fancy a nightcap.

The chosen one soon returned, walking cautiously out of the shadows. He was careful to make sure the other two did not see him. After a furtive glance up and down the empty street, he knocked on Amanda's door. Amanda opened it and ushered him in.

Face to Face

Sharkey, Sanchez, Igoravitch and Lord Milford were about to have their weekly meeting via Interface, a method by which they could all see and hear each other on huge screens in each other's home of residence.

Hank Sharkey was in his penthouse apartment in Manhattan. He was seated in his favourite power chair, drinking a martini and sitting opposite a huge screen. At his feet was his new mistress, Zaza, a beauty from Venezuela, who had given Sharkey the idea of getting rid of troublesome players by staging a tournament in Yakadakastan.

"Kill them all in the notorious Yakadakastan acid lake, darling," she had cooed in Sharkey's ear. Sharkey had nodded enthusiastically at the suggestion.

Zaza was stroking his legs as Sharkey swirled the martini around his huge glass. Outside a cold front had descended from Canada. Snow splattered on the huge windows of the penthouse.

Across the North Atlantic, Lord Milford was in the lounge of his castle in Buckinghamshire. He had just eaten lunch and was now seated in a soft, leather chair by the fireside as a butler brought him a glass of brandy on a tray. A sombre portrait of Pierre de Milford looked down at him from over the mantelpiece. A huge screen hung below the portrait.

Jose Sanchez was seated facing a big screen in the lounge of his luxury villa in Bootle on Merseyside. Thanks to an imported sun lamp, sand from a Caribbean beach, fake palm trees and blue crystals, Jose looked out on to a tropical vista instead of the grey River Mersey and black sky beyond. Jose had just finished an enjoyable after-lunch romp in his Emperor-sized bed with five wives of Merseyside FC players. He was now very relaxed as he faced the screen for the weekly meeting.

Boris Igoravitch was seated on a throne-like chair in the east wing of the presidential palace in Dakerdaker. A big screen hung from one of the walls. Various glamorous escorts attended to his needs as he relaxed while drinking a cocktail special composed of vodka, rum, gin, whisky and paraffin. Outside gunfire could be heard. His brother was executing another batch of annoying political prisoners. Boris smiled to himself. All was well in Yakadakastan.

"Good day, gentlemen," said Hank Sharkey.

Sharkey's hawk-like face appeared on all the screens. The others all gave their greetings. Sharkey continued.

"Gentleman, pay attention. We have a busy agenda today. Very busy. First, we have to finalise the arrangements for the tournament in Yakadakastan. Then we have to decide who will win what this season. And finally, we have to deal with something that's just come up. Some pesky social media crap about a disease in the stadiums. But first, the tournament. Over to you, Boris."

Boris had to break off from kissing one of his escorts.

"Ah, yes. All is good. Everyone here is excited about the tournament. Tickets have been selling well. All stadiums soon will be full. If not, the police will force people to come at gunpoint. No problems, we are ready to welcome the magical English Super League teams," said Boris.

"Excellent. And the boat trip on the lake after the tournament. Has that been arranged?" said Sharkey.

"Of course. All is good. The boat is being prepared with luxury goods, glamorous girls and the best party atmosphere. No problems," said Boris.

"Good. So, gentlemen are we all set for the tournament in a week's time?"

Jose and Lord Milford gave affirmative answers. All would be ready with regard to their respective teams.

"That's just great. I'm pleased. Now, let us see, who will win what this season?" said Sharkey.

Jose jumped in.

"I think it is time Merseyside FC won both cup and league, amigos. We have not won it for the first two seasons now," protested Jose.

"I object to that. Manchester Unity FC is expected to win three titles in a row at least. We are the biggest club after all," said Lord Milford.

"But you have won the title twice already," said Jose, annoyed at Lord Milford.

"No, no, no. It is time Birmingham Villa FC win titles and cups now. Or else I tell my brother on you," said Boris, interrupting.

There was silence for a few moments. Nobody wanted to tangle with Boris's mad, wack job of a brother.

Sharkey laughed.

"All right, gentlemen, let us see if we can sort this out. How's this. What if London City FC wins the league this year and Birmingham Villa FC the cup. How does that sound?" said Sharkey.

"But Merseyside FC need to win something this year. We expect to win, the fans expect to win," said Jose.

"And what about Manchester Unity FC. We are the best, you know," said Lord Milford, clearly agitated.

Sharkey nodded like a wise, old university professor.

"OK. Keep calm. How about this, guys. Manchester Unity FC and Merseyside FC reach the finals in the tournament in Yakadakastan. London City FC and Birmingham Villa FC will simply rollover. Lose narrowly in exciting games. Say 6-6 then a penalty shoot-out. Millions around the world will be tuned in. It's going to be big. Boris is even prepared to sacrifice his team for the good of yours. That right, Boris?" said Sharkey.

Boris was busy kissing his escort again.

"Yes, I am prepared to let one of you win final in my wonderful shit-hole of a country. If I win, they will say it rigged anyway," said Boris, laughing.

"That's right, gentlemen. If Boris's team wins on his home turf everybody will say it's rigged and we don't want that accusation levelled at us, do we?" said Sharkey.

Jose and Lord Milford nodded.

"So, best I can offer is both of your teams in the final, but my team wins the league this year and Boris's team wins the cup," said Sharkey.

"Why does your team have to win the league this year. You know we have to win three in a row," said Lord Milford.

Sharkey smiled and took a swig of his martini.

"We win this year because I say so, Lord Baby. I say so. Any problems with that?"

Nobody spoke.

"Good. We have that settled. Thank you, gentlemen, for your co-operation. I fully appreciate that. I really do. Now, finally, there is the small problem of some fruitcake out there in social media land spreading lies that there is the danger of catching a killer flu if fans go to watch ESL games. It's just new on social media," said Sharkey.

"Yes, I've heard of that," said Lord Milford, lying.

"Yes, my secretary told me. I find it annoying, amigos. Our beautiful game being tarnished by ignorant idiots," said Jose.

"You hit the nail on the head, Jose. Ignorant idiots they are. Fans who tune in around the world want to see cheering, hysterical supporters. This killer flu crap could jeopardise the size of the crowds. We haven't developed robot technology enough yet to duplicate 80,000 cheering fans. The idiots in the House of Commons do what we tell them to do and the Anti-Football Police have been magnificent. But gentlemen we need to be vigilant and remove any resistance, as we did in bagpipe land. Dissent must be crushed before it becomes a problem. Crushed, gentlemen, crushed. And I mean crushed. So, Boris, over to you, old buddy," said Sharkey.

Boris was doing more than kissing the escort. He broke off abruptly.

"Do not worry. I have a solution to the problem. Big solution. I send killers, I mean, I send men to England to deal with this minor problem. They will find who is doing this and they will make them stop, abruptly," said Boris.

"Excellent. I like the way you operate, Boris. So efficient. So, gentlemen, are there any more questions before we finish the meeting today?"

There was just silence.

"That's good. Then I will see you all in the flesh in Dakerdakar in a few days' time. Oh, and don't forget to tune in to watch the game on Tuesday morning English time. The new rules will be in force. I just can't wait to see how everybody reacts and then accepts them. Goodbye, gentlemen," said Sharkey.

Everybody said their goodbyes. Zaza kissed Sharkey.

The screens went blank.

Riots

What had looked like never happening happened. There was an anti-English Super League morning riot in England. Thousands of fans in London of the now-defunct Millwall, West Ham United, Arsenal, Chelsea, Charlton Athletic, Fulham, Crystal Palace, Brentford, Queens Park Rangers, Wimbledon and Tottenham Hotspur clubs had rioted in Trafalgar Square over the demise of their teams and the creation of the English Super League. Fans from other parts of the country were also there, demanding the return of normal football.

The rioters carried banners saying such things as:

Down With the ESL

Give Us the Money and We Will Vote For Anything as Well

We Want Real Football Not A Comedy Show

Stop changing the rules!

Surprise Us, Which Team Is Going To Win This Year?

How Much Longer Do We Have to Put Up With This Crap

What About An Offside Law For Corner Flags?

Give Us The Flu, We Love It!

I Have One Leg, Can I play For London City As Well?

Get Stuffed You Scumbags, I Want My Club Back!

The well-armed Anti-Football Police had been out in force, firstly containing the riot and secondly rounding up all the rioters. Skulls had been cracked and legs and arms had been broken. Stiff prison sentences had also been issued by kangaroo courts, with one fan being sentenced to five years detention on the Faroe Islands for wearing a 'I Love Leyton Orient' badge and burning a replica London City FC shirt.

Aside from the riot, there had been an explosion in a small rubbish bin outside a Hackney fish and chip shop. Credit for the explosion, that was no bigger than a firecracker going off in a tin can, was claimed by the Dulwich Hamlet People's Liberation Army. The DHPLA was a militant group that consisted of only of two members, Cyril and Ted Wainwright, both retired gas fitters. Twenty-five Anti-Football Police had swooped on the area and arrested them. Cyril and Ted were last seen in chains and dressed in orange overalls. Television reporters saw them being bungled into a helicopter that was headed for the dreaded Faroe Islands.

After the riots had been quelled, the Prime Minister, Tony Campbell, standing in a packed and hushed House of Commons, made a memorable speech.

"My fellow countrymen," said Campbell, incandescent with anger, "today, as we stand alone on the beaches, our backs to the wall and fronts to the front. I can only reflect, respect, rejoice and reject that this has been a dark, dull, overcast day for this wonderful country of ours. Events today reminded me of an appetising appendicectomy without an appendix. They were so terrible that they reminded me of a tearful, terrestrial terrapin on a terracotta terrace. The whole riot was an ambiguous, ambidextrous, ambitious abomination. And the explosion was more disastrous than a distasteful disaster that dissipates diagonally downwards. As Prime Minister, and mark my words, I am excruciatingly exterminated by events. I'm so exterminated that existential exercises will be exceeded to exculpate this extraordinary, extreme, extravaganza."

Members of the House of Commons exploded into applause at such a brilliant statesman-like speech. The politicians had decided that the real cause of the disturbances was not the money-gouging four-team ESL, not the banning of clubs and everyday football, not the recent ESL related bills that they had passed that could make the game a ludicrous farce, no, the real cause of the disturbances was the recent rumours on social media about a killer flu epidemic at the four ESL stadiums.

The intelligence services had been instructed to find out who had been sending out the false flu warnings on social media. Intelligence had informed the government that they had put their best hackers on the job. The prime minister had been assured it was only a matter of time before the culprits were apprehended by the Anti-Football Police.

Whoever had created the rumour had to pay. The establishment, as always, wanted revenge.

The Royal Oak, Tickhill

Billy, hunched in his big coat, was seated in his usual spot in the Royal Oak pub, but his eyes were glued to the big television screen over the bar. A packed pub was watching replays of the riots that were being shown over and over again. Mounted Anti-Football Police were seen in close-up, clubbing and hitting protesters. Blood splattered the television cameras. Roving reporters with ice-cream cone sized microphones shouted gibberish at the screen. The television then showed excerpts of the prime ministers' speech. Nobody in the bar spoke because the Anti-Football Police had informers everywhere.

Billy was soon joined by Trevor and Spud.

"The revolutions started," whispered Trevor, excitedly, as he sat next to Billy.

"Don't count on it. The AFP look as though they've snuffed it out with their usual diplomacy. Stacks have been arrested," said Billy.

"Sent 'em to the Faroe Islands. Imagine living there among icebergs and polar bears," said Spud, as he seated himself.

"Don't be daft, there's no polar bears up there, you idiot," said Trevor.

"Could be. Could be gorillas up there for all you know. What with global warming and that," said Spud.

Trevor shook his head.

"Who would ever think I'd feel sorry for Chelsea fans being beaten up," said Billy.

"And Arsenal fans," said Spud.

"I tell you; the revolution has begun. Those stupid laws they passed the other day were the icing on the cake. We can't take any more crap," said Trevor.

More pictures of the riots flashed on the screen. The Anti-Football Police were seen in close-up, smashing up banners and dragging off protesters. Some Millwall fans got in a few punches against a loan AFP officer. The crowd around the bar gave a muted cheer.

"Did all of you send out that stuff about the flu infecting the stadiums?" said Trevor.

"Not yet, but, but I will, I will," said Spud, keenly watching the screen.

"Me too. When I get home. I will, I'll get the laptop buzzing," said Billy.

"Same here, just been too busy," said Trevor.

The group around the bar gasped as the television showed an Anti-Football Police officer kicking a teenage girl wearing a Fulham scarf. A demonstrator wearing a Charlton Athletic T-shirt tried to escape but he was rugby tackled by an AFP officer and then kicked in the head by another. The crowd around the bar groaned.

For a brief moment the men watching went silent, distracted by a shapely female AFP officer dressed in a tight, low-cut black uniform. She had short black hair and bright red lips. The officer ruthlessly wielded a baton as she clubbed several female demonstrators.

The words 'hot sexy babe' were spoken by those closest to the television set.

"Hey, where's Amanda?" said Spud, breaking the ambience and looking around.

"Dunno. She's not here. I thought she was with you two?" said Billy.

"We haven't seen her," said Trevor.

"Well, she should be here any time. That's what we agreed the other night, to meet here," said Spud.

"You're right. Right here. I wonder where she could be, then?" said Billy, reaching for his beer.

"Yeah, I wonder," said Trevor, his eyes glued to the violence on the television screen.

Amanda Escapes

Amanda knew it hadn't been a good idea to invite Billy back to her flat the moment she opened the front door to let him in. It was just that, well, she fancied some sex and Billy was looking far more appealing than Spud or Trevor that night. Which didn't say a lot for Spud and Trevor.

Not that it was all bad. Billy did perform quite well considering he was a bit overweight, overexcited and totally out of practice. And the romp between the sheets did relax Amanda a little. But afterwards, Billy wanted to hang around and tell Amanda about his failed love life and his on-again, off-again romance with a barmaid in Barnsley. He even showed Amanda photographs of her, pulling a pint in the Dog and Duck. The endless waffle all became too much in the end, especially when Billy wanted more sex. So, after a few harsh words, Amanda bungled him out into the street. It was three in the morning.

Besides, Amanda had things to do. After Billy had gone, she pulled out her laptop and began to spread the word that the four ESL stadiums were infected with a deadly flu virus. She logged into every social site she knew and typed away deep into the night, giving graphic details of the symptoms under a variety of false names and how deadly the disease was and how easy it was to catch it.

By early morning she was exhausted. She had posted hundreds of messages. She was hopeful that the word was out and that social media would do its magic and spread the word far and wide. She put the laptop aside and staggered to bed. The riots in London occurred some five hours later while Amanda was in a deep sleep.

Amanda woke at around four o'clock in the afternoon. It was already getting dark and she wondered for a moment where she was. After collecting her thoughts and getting her bearings, she dressed and vaguely recalled the sex with Billy, the hard hours spent banging away on her laptop and the sleep that had engulfed her. There was also something else nagging her. Yes, the meeting at the Royal Oak with the others.

For a second she thought about Spud and Billy. Would Billy say anything? Would he brag about what had happened between the sheets? She tossed over thoughts until objective analysis became too complicated for her fogged brain. Amanda slipped on her big hooded jacket and opened the front door. It was then that she noticed something odd.

Two black vans were parked close to the block of flats. She knew that nobody in the area had vans like these. They were too big, too official-looking, too expensive, too important. The windows were blacked out, so she couldn't see anybody inside. She recalled that she had seen this make of vehicle before. On television during the Scottish riots in Glasgow. The vans had been everywhere. The same vans that had the Anti-Football Police tumbling out of them with billy clubs. If sleep had been holding her back it quickly disappeared. Amanda sensed danger. She back peddled and discreetly closed the door and rushed back inside.

She went to the bedroom and quickly packed clothes, her laptop and some toiletries in her backpack. She also grabbed her old sleeping bag and headed for the back door.

Amanda paused for thought. Whoever was in the vans was probably studying the flats, looking at the collection of small satellite dishes attached like warts to the side of the building. Fortunately, there were sixteen flats in the block. Maybe that would confuse whoever was in the vehicles long enough for Amanda to make a decent escape.

Amanda checked her pockets for her wallet and phone. She then slipped out of the back door, crossed a small lane and disappeared down a dark, cobbled alley.

An Angry Phone Call

Hank Sharkey had just seen a replay of the television footage of the riots in London. Seething with anger, he immediately got on the phone and called the British Prime Minister, Tony Campbell, on his special hotline.

"Listen, half-wit, what's going on over there?" yelled Sharkey, as Campbell took the call.

"Nothing to worry about, Hank. Just some hooligans having a bit of fun," said Campbell.

"Fun? You call that fun? They are trying to trash the brand. I have never seen anything like it. Now put a stop to this crap and have those peasants arrested and sent to some flea pit. I don't want to see any more riots and banners waving around in front of television cameras. Is that understood?" growled Sharkey.

"Yes, yes, no problem, we have the situation under control," said Campbell.

"You'd better. Don't forget you have a stake in all this soccer crap. I don't pay you thousands of hard-earned dollars a week to let half-wits run around the street holding up abusive banners. If you can't control these morons than perhaps there is someone in your House of Commons who can!"

Campbell swallowed hard. He liked being the prime minister, but he knew that Sharkey had the power to change that.

"Don't worry, Hank. It's nothing. Nothing at all. A mere blip. The Anti-Football Police have arrested most of the ring leaders already. All is quiet. Everything is back to normal," said Campbell.

"Is it really? What about this killer flu crap that's going around on social media? Haven't you got the balls to close down all social media in your poxy little island? Put up a massive firewall or something? That will stop all this crap from happening in the first place!"

Campbell had seriously thought about having a huge firewall to stop social media. But he had only thought about it. Payments into his bank account by search engine and internet providers had been enough to kill the idea. For now.

"We, we are thinking of putting up a firewall," said Campbell.

"Thinking is no good! Thinking is bad for you. Action is what is needed. Action! I didn't get where I am today by just thinking! Look, the Chinese can put up a firewall, so why can't you idiots?"

"As I say, we are thinking about it."

"That's not good enough in my book. So, have you caught the scumbag who put out these lies on social media about the killer flu yet?"

Campbell re-crossed his legs.

"Not yet, no," said Campbell.

"Not yet, no! Am I hearing this right? What sort of cockamamie government are you running, fat boy?" said Hank.

Campbell took exception to the fat boy remark, but thought it best not to argue.

"Look, we are hot on the culprit's trail. Our IT specialists have zeroed in on where the information came from and a crack squad of the Anti-Football Police are heading there as we speak. It's just a matter of time before we make an arrest, Hank. A matter of time."

"A matter of time? It had better be. I want the culprit hung, drawn and quartered, like they used to in the good old days. Strung up on a scaffold. Left to rot for all to see. That's the way to deal with these cretins. Kill them off. Leave them hanging like dog meat. Don't you realise that these fools are messing with my investment. The English Super League is one of the finest scams for gouging money out of mug punters that I have ever come across. Now find that piece of scum and have them executed. And no sending them to some poxy island or prison camp. I want the criminal dead. As in dead, dead! Got that? And I want it to be seen on television in prime time. Close-ups, the lot. That will be an example to all those who mess with Hank Sharkey. Have you got that, knucklehead?"

Again, Campbell swallowed hard.

"Yes, yes. I understand your frustration, Hank. But don't worry. We will find the culprit and punish him."

"Good. Then get to it!"

Hank Sharkey slammed down the phone and swore. Zaza approached and stood behind him, gently rubbing the base of his neck.

"Do not worry, darling. You are getting all tense for nothing," said Zaza.

Suddenly, Sharkey felt calm and more relaxed. But this state of relaxation didn't last long. A text from Jose Sanchez came through on his phone to tell Sharkey that so far, the stadium for Tuesday mornings impending big game between Merseyside FC and Manchester Unity FC was under half full. Usually, it was seething with fans by now.

Sharkey got back on to the phone.

"Jose, what's happening over there?" said Sharkey.

"Hey, amigo, the stadium is only half full and we are nearing kick-off. The flu thing has scared fans away, I think. It a big game, too," said Sanchez.

"We can't have that. A worldwide television broadcast showing the stadium only half-full will be a disaster. Look, get some cardboard dummies in there fast. Drag people into the stadium if you have to. Get them to magnify the sound. Get some crowd cheering overlay sounds on the broadcast. And get the idiots behind the cameras to concentrate the crowd into small groups, to make it look full. Get the crowd to squeeze up. Got that?"

"See, amigo. Squeeze up. Sound magnified. I'll get on to it immediately," said Sanchez.

"Good. Oh, and you win tonight. About 4-3 will do. Make it exciting. The new rules should help. Lots of goals. Lots of action. Let's see some blood. Let's show the world what a great, honest product the English Super League is. Got that, Jose?"

"See, amigo. Good, we win 4-3. Milford will not like that."

"Screw Milford. You win. That's it."

Sharkey slammed down the phone. Zaza began to rub his neck again, but Sharkey couldn't relax. Not this time. He just wanted to get his hands on the person who had invented the killer flu story.

Billy's Place

After hanging around the Royal Oak for a few hours, Billy, Spud and Trevor reluctantly drifted over to Billy's flat to watch the Merseyside FC v Manchester Unity FC game on television. Normally they wouldn't watch such a game but they were interested in the crowd size and the effect the new rule changes would have.

The lads seated themselves on Billy's crumbling, flaky couch, popped open some beers and settled down to watch the screen in front of them. The kick-off was imminent. A jaded team photo of Rotherham United players from 1969 looked down at them from the cracked wall behind the screen.

The game would be played at the New Merseyside Stadium, a colossal extravaganza of a stadium that seated over 80,000 fans. It was situated only a mile away from Liverpool's old Anfield Stadium that was now used for the collection of rubbish in plastic bags.

At first glance, the crowd seemed just as big as ever. The chanting sounded delirious, as fans from both sides waved banners and flags. But on closer inspection, all was not as it should be. There were obvious gaps in the crowd.

"Hey, look, it's only half-full. Less than 30,000 at a guess," said Trevor, excitedly.

The others craned forward to get a better look.

"Yeah, look, the AFP scum are forcing the fans together so as to make it look crowded," said Spud.

Spud was right. Anti-Football Police could clearly be seen herding both sets of fans together. The gaps in the crowd became more evident when a cameraman inadvertently pointed his camera to the upper stands.

"See that, nobody is up there," said Billy.

"It's half-empty. Bloody empty! That's great!" said Spud.

"Normally it would be full. Full of nutcases. Fantastic! Looks like the killer flu thing is working," said Trevor.

"Brilliant! Bloody brilliant!" said Billy.

The lads simultaneously took a swig of beer.

"This is brilliant!" said Billy.

"Yeah, but are we going to keep watching this shit?" said Trevor.

"Yeah, to see how those stupid new rules play out. It could be a fiasco. What with the crowd being small as well," said Billy.

"Yeah, I agree, leave it on, we could be witnessing history," said Spud.

"Yeah, all right," said Trevor.

The three stayed glued to the screen as the teams ran out. Merseyside FC in red, Manchester Unity FC in blue. The commentators, chosen for their overexcitability and lack of knowledge about the game, waffled on to tell viewers that Merseyside FC would line up in the usual 3-2-1-1-2-1 formation plus one extra player in disguise, while Manchester Unity FC would be testing a radical, innovative 4-4-2 system.

Thanks to the new legislation passed recently in the House of Commons, Merseyside FC would have an extra player on the field disguised in a Manchester Unity FC shirt, while all players would be immune from offside. There was also a chance the supplementary goal rule would be used, along with the use of a cardboard referee and the sending off/not sending off rule. For extra entertainment, a clown was scheduled to appear on the pitch during play. It promised to be an unusual game.

Merseyside FC attacked from the kick-off and scored an early goal when their in-disguise player, wearing a Manchester Unity FC shirt and a Batman face mask, headed in from a corner. Manchester Unity FC quickly got back into the game when their top striker, Carlos O' Jones, tapped in a cross from the left. 1-1.

The game looked like a normal game for several minutes. But that all changed halfway through the first half when the in-disguise Merseyside FC player in the Manchester Unity FC shirt and Batman mask, burst into life, dribbled all the Manchester Unity FC defence and scored a second goal. He then grabbed a Manchester Unity FC player, body-slammed him to the ground and demanded a submission.

In anger, a Manchester Unity FC player stomped on the in-disguise player and pulled off his Batman mask and ripped it to shreds. The player was immediately sent off for violent conduct against a superhero costume. Seconds later the sent-off player, Hercules Brown, was allowed back on the field again in strict accordance with the sent off/not sent off rule. Brown then punched the referee, knocking him out cold. The referee was carried off and was immediately replaced by a cardboard cut-out referee, who refereed the game without further incident until half-time. 2-1 to Merseyside FC.

Billy, Trevor and Spud re-supplied themselves with beer for the second half.

"What a mess," said Trevor.

"It's a laugh though," said Spud.

"A cardboard referee refereeing the game. Unbelievable!" said Billy.

"A player in a Batman mask! Wrestling on the pitch! A player sent off then comes back on again! The referee knocked cold! Unbelievable!" said Trevor.

A new, obviously human referee, was evident as the players came out of the dressing rooms for the second half.

Manchester Unity FC attacked from the kick-off and scored an equaliser when a wayward shot hit O'Jones on the back of the head and flew into the top corner of the goal. 2-2. O'Jones was knocked unconscious, but he was left on the pitch, stretched out on the six-yard line for the rest of the game. A clown then appeared on the pitch near the centre circle and juggled some tennis balls in the air before exiting doing cartwheels.

Merseyside FC hit back, when their in-disguise player, now wearing a Zorro mask, scored with a deliberate hand-ball worthy of a basketball player. 3-2 to Merseyside FC. Manchester Unity FC players loudly protested the awarding of the goal and crowded around the referee, who, in anger at being questioned, waved his hands around hysterically to draw attention to himself and then punished Manchester Unity FC further by pointing to the penalty spot twice.

Fernando Wilson scored easily from the penalty spot when the Manchester Unity FC goalkeeper refused to stand in the goal and went off the field to eat a pie. Wilson scored easily again with the second penalty with the goalkeeper still off the field taking part in a hot chocolate commercial. 5-2 to Merseyside FC.

When Manchester Unity FC players continued to vehemently protest the referee announced he had awarded two supplementary goals and a half supplementary goal to Merseyside FC for persistent arguing by Manchester Unity FC players. The score was now 7 and one-half goals to Merseyside FC and 2 goals to Manchester Unity FC.

Manchester Unity FC did get a consolation goal near the end when a wild shot hit the still unconscious O'Jones on the head again and, wrong-footing the goalkeeper, trickled over the line. The final score was Merseyside FC 7 and one-half goals to Manchester Unity FC's 3 goals.

"What a cock-up," said Trevor, laughing.

"Absolute crap! A total comedy show," said Billy, cracking up.

"But listen to the crowd," said Spud.

Sure enough, the crowd could be seen and heard cheering fanatically as the players trudged off the field. The co-commentators were face-to-camera, talking forty to the dozen about what an exciting game it had been. In the background, O'Jones could be seen being carried off on a stretcher, while the referee was surrounded by Manchester Unity FC playing staff. An angry altercation looked about to break out near the players' tunnel. Then the players, officials and stadium dramatically disappeared from the screen as a 'Breaking News' flash replaced the farce that had been a football match.

Billy was just about to turn off the TV with the remote when pictures of the outside of Amanda's block of flats hit the screen.

"Hey, look, that's Amanda's place," said Billy.

"Yeah, you're right, it is!" said Spud.

The screen was showing a commentator eagerly announcing a fatal shooting at a block of flats in Tickhill. Shouting excitedly into a microphone the size of a house brick, the commentator stated that five Anti-Football Police officers had been ambushed on the stairwell of a block of flats by three unknown gunmen with one of the AFP officers being fatally injured.

"Holy shit!" said Billy, open-mouthed.

The three friends stared transfixed at the TV.

What the hell was going on?

Another Angry Phone Call

Sharkey, with Zaza seated next to him, were in Sharkey's private helicopter. The couple were making their way to La Guardia airport in order to board Sharkey's private jet. They were on their way to Yakadakastan for the Inter-Championship Euro-Asia Cup-Cup, as the four-team tournament in Dakerdaker had been called. But Sharkey was confused over the media's reaction to last nights' game between Merseyside FC and Manchester Unity FC.

Early news bulletins from the United Kingdom had described the game as a comical shambles and castigated the new rules. More worrisome for Sharkey was that the crowd was very small, down by some 45,000 fans. But in America, CCNN and Jackal Sports thought the game was brilliant and just what was needed to liven up the boring game that was soccer.

Sharkey decided that he knew who to blame for the abject reports from the United Kingdom. He tapped out a number on his phone.

"What the hell is going on over there?" said Sharkey.

"What's the problem, Hank?" said Tony Campbell, who had just got out of bed at No 10.

"Don't give me that I-don't-know-what's-going-on-crap! It's all over your news bulletins. Fiasco of a game! Football

76

or farce! Didn't you explain the new rules to the public and media over there before the game?"

"We tried to, but I thought it best to let things just run and..."

"And what? You have no idea, have you? Just let it drift, huh? Is that how you operate? Well, let me tell you, that's not how I operate. No sir. If you'd explained things before the game to those morons who follow this stupid sport then maybe we would not have become a laughing stock."

"But, Hank, it was always going to be difficult for fans to swallow supplementary goals, players not being offside, twelve players on one team, half a goal been given, players wrestling in superhero masks, players sent off and being allowed back on again and cardboard referees. And a clown on the pitch. For heaven's sake!"

"Nonsense! They are sensible rule changes. You passed them in your House of Crap! They'll get used to it. It went down well over here. Really big time. Went down big on all the cable channels. Soccer is exciting again! Soccer is now a game for Americans! That's what they are saying over here! Jackal Sports was effusive!" said Sharkey.

"Yes, yes, I've heard that last night's' game was well received in America, Hank."

"It sure was. The rule changes are a big success here. Just what a boring game needed. There have been changes in your game before. I know this because I've read all about it. Allowing substitutes, having crossbars and goal netting. Fiddling with that damn offside crap that I can never understand. Not allowing goalkeepers to pick up the ball from a pass back. Red and yellow cards. Marking changes on the pitch. Spraying foam on the pitch. Penalty shootouts. See, these were all new rules that the fans now take as gospel. It's just a matter of time before they accept my new rules. You understand me?"

"Yes, yes, but those rule changes you just mentioned were over time, over years, and they were not as radical as the new rules you have introduced," said Campbell.

"Utter crap! Now listen! They'll accept these new rules and all the other new rules I have in mind. Got that?"

Campbell gulped. What other new rules?

"Err, what, what other new rules have you in mind, Hank?" said Campbell, nervously.

"What have I in mind? I'll tell you what I have in mind. I want more and more action. Less of this boring kicking balls to each other. I want bigger goals, forty feet by forty feet. That way we will have more goals scored. More excitement. No goalkeepers either. Waste of space and money if you ask me. Two or maybe three balls on the pitch at the same time. That will make it very interesting. Simulated earthquakes during games to make it more difficult. Advertisements during games before every throw-in. Three teams playing on the same pitch instead of two. Fighting to be allowed. Lots of fighting. Lots of blood. Tag team wrestling. More circus clowns on the field. Maybe some sea lions performing tricks. Teams all in the same-coloured shirts to create confusion. Different markings on the pitch. A huge quadrilateral shape instead of that big, dumb circle in the middle. I love quadrilaterals. What I have in mind is mind-boggling, Tony, mind-boggling. Soccer will never be the same again!"

Inwardly, Tony Campbell groaned. He could see scores of 25-18 and cage fighters, wrestlers, clowns, sea lions and maybe elephants on the field. Sharkey's insane ideas were a recipe for mass chaos and ridicule.

"Look, look, Hank, I think it best we stay as we are for now. This season at least. Let the new rules sink in. Let them be digested by the fans," said Campbell.

"Utter crap! I move fast. Very fast. That's my style. No marking time. I want these new rules brought in by next month. I want them passed in your dumb parliament or else you will no longer be prime minister! Got that! Also, have you made any headway on tracking down the perpetrator of the killer flu lies?"

Campbell had just read a report on an overnight incident while he was propped up in bed.

"Well, yes, well, we, we tracked the source to a block of flats in the north, but AFP officers were ambushed by some gunmen. One of the Anti-Football Police officers described them as East European looking. Obviously, they were the culprits and they were hiding out in the flats. But they escaped. But we are on to them," said Campbell.

Sharkey was not sure how to digest this information. Didn't Boris say he would send guys to deal with the killer flu source? Maybe the two-armed groups got in each other's way and someone fired first?

"Yeah, OK. That's good to hear. Good to hear. See to it. And don't delay. I want those responsible caught."

Campbell was relieved to have escaped another verbal blast.

"No problem, Hank. We are on to it," said Campbell.

There was a pause on the line. Zaza was stroking Sharkey's left thigh.

"Oh, by the way. Pack your suitcase, I'm going to pick you up," said Sharkey.

Campbell gulped.

"Pick me up?"

"Yeah. I think a nice holiday for you in Yakadakastan would do you good. You can watch the tournament. Maybe present the losers medals. There are some fabulous women there. Hey, there could be some trade deals on hand as well. Some good publicity for you. Hell, I think you could do with some."

"But, but look, over here we have a grand visit by the prime minister of Greenland to attend to, he will be discussing climate change and the iceberg crises."

Recently, a giant iceberg had broken off from the Greenland ice pack and smashed into a beach in the Bahamas.

"The prime minister of Greenland also wants to discuss building Club Med-style resorts on the Greenland coast," said Campbell.

Sharkey was not impressed.

"Listen to me! Stuff the prime minister of goddamn Greenland! All that climate change, iceberg crap! There's no money in climate change! No money in icebergs! Club Meds in Greenland? Are you insane? Listen, my jet will be at Heathrow's private jet terminal in a few hours' time. Got that? Now be there," said Sharkey, as he hung up.

Campbell, hands all a tremble, put the phone down and wondered what he should wear in such a wild place as Yakadakastan.

Zaza gave Sharkey a kiss on the forehead. She knew how to destress him. As he eased back in his seat in the helicopter, all that Hank Sharkey could see was Tony Campbell, drink in hand, relaxed and laughing, deep in the bowels of a luxury yacht in the middle of a tranquil lake. Sharkey smiled at the thought as Zaza kissed him again.

Amanda's Hideaway

Surprisingly the night had been mild. The rain that had threatened earlier thankfully had not arrived. Amanda's only problem during the night had been clumps of sharp, dead holly leaves sticking into her every time she turned over in her sleeping bag.

After slipping away from her flat, Amanda had a caught a bus to Sheffield and then another to the Gleadless Valley Estate on the southern part of the city. The council estate had been carved into some ancient woodland some sixty years ago and had won a European award for diverse architecture. Her Aunt Lucy had lived there for several years in a maisonette on Ironside Road. Amanda had spent many a happy childhood visiting her and playing in the adjoining woods during long summers. It was this childhood knowledge of the woods that she now put to use.

In the top corner of the woods were some thick holly bushes. They had always been useful to hide in when playing games as a child. It was this clump of bushes, shaped like a den, that Amanda now found herself sitting under.

Amanda had arrived at the woods in the dead of night. Fortunately, she had a torch and found her way by instinct to the bushes after climbing over the steel fence that surrounded the wood. The night had promised to be long, but surprisingly she had fallen asleep quickly and woke to find weak daylight shafting in through the foliage.

Pulling out her phone she hesitated before turning it on. She checked the time and then the BBC app. Three items down she was shocked to see her own face accompanying a short news item.

Amanda Sarah Harper, 31, is wanted in connection with spreading false news on social media about a flu epidemic in the English Super League stadiums. This false news badly affected the attendance at the Merseyside FC v Manchester Unity FC game on Tuesday morning. The Anti-Football Police and the Metro Police are anxious to interview her. A reward will soon be offered for any information as to her whereabouts.

Amanda turned off the phone. She was wanted by the authorities and her face was out there. Shit! It was a new experience for her. Amanda was now a wanted criminal. She could only assume that her face would be plastered all over social media as well as the few newspapers that still existed. That meant that it probably wasn't safe to venture out of the woods and into the big world again.

Amanda sat on the sleeping bag in the den and gave the situation some deep thought. At first, she was shocked to see the news item. The item on the app meant that life would never be the same. No longer could she wander the streets without being noticed. No longer could she venture into the Royal Oak and have a quiet drink with her mates. Amanda suddenly realised she was a fugitive. A wanted woman.

For a minute the thought of being on the run, possibly the most wanted woman in the country, excited her. Fame at last! But reality didn't take long to kick in. If caught she would be punished severely. She knew that. So, what was the future? Prison? Sent to the Faroe Islands? Whatever it was, her future did not look rosy.

Amanda's dire thoughts regarding her future were interrupted by hunger pangs. The chocolate bars she had bought at the bus station had all been eaten last night before she had clambered into the wood. But the good news was that the nearest shops were not far away. She knew from past experience that there was a small cluster of shops just behind the two big tower blocks on the nearby Herdings Estate. They were tantalisingly only a short walking distance from where she was hiding.

Amanda checked her wallet. She had enough cash on her to last for a few more days. She wanted to avoid any ATMs or paying for anything with her credit card. That would leave a trail, one the authorities would soon pick up on. While she had cash and she was in hiding she assured herself that she was safe. Nobody knew where she was. She had turned off her phone and there had hardly been anyone on the buses last night. She was also certain that nobody had seen her slip into the woods during the night.

Hunger dictated Amanda's decision making. She decided to make her way to the shops. She unpacked her backpack of clothes and placed them inside her sleeping bag and left it in the holly bush den. Amanda pulled the hood on her jacket as far as she could over her face, picked up her now empty backpack and set off through the woods.

What Amanda didn't know was that during the short interlude when she had looked at the BBC app, her phone had sent out a signal, a faint ping, but one that had been picked up by an Anti-Football Police surveillance van in the small town of Dronfield, just south of Sheffield.

As Amanda clambered over the metal railings surrounding the wood, other Anti-Football Police vans were alerted and began heading to the Gleadless Valley. The estate, which had long been neglected, was now very important.

The Boys from Brazil

Spud, Billy and Trevor were seated in The Rio Cafe some yards away from the Royal Oak. It was far too early for the heavy stuff. Something more brain-stimulating was required. They were seated at a window table so that they could have a firsthand view of the gloomy main street. They ordered coffee as rain dribbled down the cafe's front window.

Through the course of the morning all of them had been trying to make contact with Amanda. So far, no luck.

"She must have turned it off," said Spud.

"Well, that's obvious," said Billy.

"She never turns it off. Something's wrong," said Trevor.

"Course something's wrong. What do you think that was all about on the news? They are after her for the flu stuff. You saw how the crowd was down at the game. Hey, it was good, that. Crap crowd." said Billy.

The waitress arrived with three cups of coffee on a tray. She placed the steaming liquid in front of each of them then left.

"She's new," said Trevor, as he watched the waitress walk away.

"Never mind her. Concentrate on Amanda," said Billy.

Spud cleared his throat.

"Look, she's either been arrested or, or, she's in hiding somewhere," said Spud.

"Let's hope she's in hiding," said Trevor.

"Yeah, she's in hiding. I know she will be," said Spud.

"But where?" said Billy.

"Why don't we go around to the flat. See if she's there. That would sort out everything," said Spud.

Billy looked at Trevor.

"Not a good idea, Spud. Not a good idea at all. See they might be watching the place. To see if she turns up. Surveillance, they call it. Anyone else turning up at her place could be questioned or arrested. Or even worse. Best we keep away," said Billy.

Spud nodded. He didn't want to end up in detention on the Faroe Islands.

"So, what do we do, then?" said Spud.

The lads paused to drink their coffee.

"If they'd caught her it would be on the news. An example, like. They wouldn't keep it quiet," said Billy.

"Yeah, you're right. So, what you're saying is, that she's still free. In hiding, but free?" said Trevor.

"Yeah, that's what I'm saying," said Billy.

There was a pause for thought.

"So, if she's free, where is she then?" said Spud.

The lads had another drink. The rain was getting heavier.

"I think I might know," said Trevor.

"Oh, yeah, where is she then?" said Spud.

"It's not one of your daft ideas is it?" said Billy.

"What do you mean, daft ideas? Look, I really think I know where she might be," said Trevor.

"Yeah, all right, where then, where is she, Einstein?" said Billy.

"Yeah, where is she?" said Spud.

Trevor glanced out of the cafe window. He then turned back to face his mates. He furrowed his brow. He had seen tough guy actors do this in countless films.

"Have you both got enough bus fare to get to Sheffield?" said Trevor.

Bargains

Amanda had taken a small wire basket on entering the supermarket and was now busy filling it with items that her new life demanded. She filled the basket with fresh fruit, sandwiches, small cakes, packets of biscuits, bottled water, tinned meat, baked beans, a tin opener, cheese and some small bread rolls. She also bought toothpaste, a toothbrush, four toilet rolls, shampoo and soap. She paid cash to the disinterested check-out girl and carefully packed the newly purchased goods into her backpack.

At a small cafe next door, she bought a coffee and a custard tart and seated herself on a small wall near the tower blocks. She tilted her head to catch the suns weak rays. As far as she could tell nobody at the shops had recognised her.

Life in dystopian England was becoming impossible, thought Amanda. She knew that the fake flu rumour would not last long. Soon, it would be disproved and the stadiums would be full again of cheering lunatics. She hadn't seen last night's game so she had no idea what the game had looked like, what with the new rules and the half-empty stadium. So, what more could be done?

Nothing. There was really nothing more she or her mates could do as individuals. As long as the ESL had the loyalty of the well-paid Anti-Football Police, most of whom were former football hooligans, riots by substantial numbers of protesters could be easily crushed. Fake flu epidemics would be an irritant but they would not bring down the whole structure: the ESL, the fools in the House of Commons, the wealthy mega-owners, the Anti-Football Police and the mad regime that was now England, with its posh-only work laws. And now the odious regime was out to get her.

And why was she worried about football? She couldn't even be bothered about it most of the time when all was normal. Football! What was football? Just a bunch of blokes in shorts with a number on their backs running around a field chasing a ball and kicking it into a net. Bloody stupid! It was only because of her mates that she had got involved in this in the first place. Or maybe not. Maybe she just loved challenging the system.

Amanda finished eating the custard tart and drank her coffee. She had decided it was time to get out of England. Yes, get up and go. A few months ago, she had seriously thought of enrolling at a Posh Talk College. This was a college where you were taught a posh accent so that you could get a job. Thousands of them had sprung up all over the country after the legislation had been passed guaranteeing jobs to people who talked posh. But the fees were too high and besides, she was proud of her Yorkshire accent.

After dismissing enrolment in a Posh Talk College, Amanda had thought of starting a new life elsewhere. Secretly she had given the idea serious thought over the past few weeks. Emigrate to New Zealand, Canada or Australia. Hadn't Uncle Ron always said that England was rotten to the core, that it was a system designed for the rich, the wealthy, the landed and the privileged?

The Deep State Uncle Ron had called it. "It's rotten, Amanda, it's rotten. The government, the army, the police, and the law is there to protect them, the privileged few. Not us. Them. There are so few of them so they need all that state structure to protect them from us, the majority. They fool us with nationalism and patriotism," he had said. Amanda had a suspicion that Uncle Ron had been right after all.

Amanda picked up her bulging backpack and headed to the woods. She passed the tower blocks and walked down the grassy slope. Any faint hint that the sun might break through had gone. The sky was now iron grey, the wind cold and biting. Before going into the wood, she hesitated to check to see if she was being observed. And if she was, so what? Yeah, so what. She was just somebody climbing the railings and entering the wood. Surely, it happened all the time. People taking a short cut.

Amanda climbed the metal rail fencing without any trouble. With her backpack hanging from one shoulder, Amanda made her way towards the holly bushes. The wind had picked up and was making a rushing sound as it speared through the bare branches of the tall trees. As she made her way along the faintly outlined path, she thought about what she was going to eat first. The biscuits? The cakes?

Finally, she reached the entrance to her temporary home and crawled into the shelter, dragging the backpack with her. But there was something wrong. Very wrong. Her sleeping bag, that had been stuffed with her clothes, had gone.

Lord Milford Makes a Stand

"It was a humiliation, Hank, a bloody humiliation!" said Lord Milford.

An agitated Lord Milford had buttonholed Hank Sharkey in the luxury lounge at Heathrow's private jet terminal prior to their flights to Dakerdaker.

"Look, losing 7 and a half goals to 3 was ludicrous! Totally ludicrous. Half a goal. Penalties given for nothing. Players sent off then coming back on again. Cardboard referees. A player in a mask. A clown on the pitch juggling balls! Wrestling! I ask you, Hank, wrestling! What is going on in your mind?" said Lord Milford.

Sharkey, seated on a large settee with Zaza cuddled up close to him, laughed.

"I've been talking to Jose. He's not happy as well," said Lord Milford.

"Get used to it, Lord Baby, get used to it. There's more where that came from," said Sharkey.

Lord Milford paced up and down.

"Get used to it? There's more? Are you totally insane! You've ruined the game. Do you know that? You have ruined the game. We'll all be a laughing stock. There's bound to be a revolution now!"

Sharkey and Zaza enjoyed a long kiss before Sharkey replied.

"Look, Lord Baby. Calm down. Cool it. It went down well stateside. Very well. Face it, your soccer shit is boring. Pass here, pass there, no goals for ages. Oh, man. How can you watch such crap? When I invented this English Super League stuff, I was determined to change the game forever. I'm a game changer! Hey, I like that description, don't you, Zaza? Game changer."

Zaza nodded then kissed Sharkey again with her amazing lips.

"But, Hank, the game is the game. It's the world's most popular game because of what it is. Low scoring, fast, exciting. It's not basketball or baseball. It's football."

"It's crap," said Sharkey, before kissing Zaza again.

Lord Milford inwardly groaned.

"Look, if we play the game to those rules in Yakerdakerstan we are finished. The whole world will laugh at us. The crowds you saw in that London riot will be nothing compared to what is coming. It nearly happened before you know," said Lord Milford.

Sharkey turned away from Zaza's open, lipstick coated mouth.

"When did it nearly happen before, Lord Baby?"

"It did. In 1381."

"1381? What, at half-past one or something?" said Sharkey, his left hand now on one of Zaza's large breasts.

"No, no. In the year 1381. It was called the Peasants Revolt. They nearly killed everybody."

"What do you mean, they nearly killed everybody?"

93

"Everybody who was important. Aristocrats, archbishops, mayors, anybody who was important. The peasants were upset about taxation. A poll tax and other taxes levied on them by the rich for wars in France. They almost killed the king as well. Total revolution."

Sharkey laughed.

"But we are not taxing anybody, Lord Baby. I hate taxes as much as those peasants did."

"I'm not talking about taxation, Hank. I'm just saying that if people get really upset, and I mean really upset about something, then they will do drastic things."

"So, you think it might happen again, Lord Baby?"

Lord Milford nodded.

"It could, it could. But it won't happen if we stop messing with the football rules. Having just four teams is hard enough to contain without changing the rules as well, especially the stupid, idiotic, insane rules you have brought in."

Sharkey was off the couch in a flash. He grabbed Lord Milford by the throat and slammed him hard against the wall.

"Listen, Englishman. I do what I do. Understand? Nobody stops me and nobody insults me. The ESL is my baby. Mine. My money helps to pay off all those useless politicians in your House of Commons. My money helps to pay the exorbitant salaries of your Anti-Football Police. Understand? You and the other two jerks are just along for the ride. The money ride. Big money. What I do with my product is my business. Got that? I said, have you got that?"

Lord Milford tried to nod his head. His face was severely bright red and bloated.

Zaza slipped off the couch and in her long, tight dress, sashayed over to the two men.

"Leave him, darling, he is not worth it," said Zaza, stroking Sharkey's arm with her long, manicured fingers.

Sharkey increased his vice-like grip on Lord Milford's throat before releasing him. Lord Milford collapsed in a heap.

Sharkey straightened up his clothing as Zaza stroked Sharkey's face. Sharkey paced then paused and took some deep breaths. He was doing some deep thinking. There was a long uncomfortable silence. Lord Milford moaned. Zaza moved away and kept her eyes on Sharkey as she applied a coat of lipstick to her full lips. The rooms electric clock hummed.

"All right, Lord Baby. All right. Have it your way for now. For now. We play the tournament in Dakerdaker under normal soccer rules. But afterwards, afterwards, changes will be made, more changes, more changes and even more changes until I'm satisfied. Understand? And they will be permanent changes. Forever. In perpetuity. You got that, Lord Baby?"

The crumpled figure of Lord Milford mumbled something. Sharkey kicked him then laughed.

"Good. I'm glad we see things the same. Now, I have a plane to catch. The Prime Minister of the United Kingdom is already seated on my private jet enjoying my hospitality. I mustn't keep him waiting. And, I believe you also have a plane to catch as well, Lord Baby?"

Lord Milford grunted.

"That's good. Very good. I'll see you in Dakerdaker, Lord Baby. And do straighten that tie of yours, you look so, so un-Lordly."

Zaza threw back her head and gave a throaty laugh. Sharkey kissed her. Sharkey and Zaza, arm in arm, exited the lounge, leaving Lord Milford to stagger to his feet and straighten his clothing.

A Walk in the Woods

"So, genius, how do you know she's here?" said Billy.

Billy, Spud and Trevor had just entered the woods near Ironside Road on the Gleadless Valley Estate. They had crossed the small stream and were now climbing upwards towards the holly bushes with Trevor leading the way.

"We were talking one night in the Royal Oak. She told me about this place. See, I said that I had relatives here as well. Over on Gaunt Road. Mum's sister. Auntie Clare. In summer we would come over from Tickhill to see her. Me and my cousin, Alan, would come to this wood to play as it was safer. Amanda said that she played in the same wood as a kid as well. She said that she felt safe playing in the holly bushes. There was something about a ghost in the Gaunt Road woods that scared us kids off from playing there so we came here, this side of the estate," said Trevor.

"A ghost?" said Spud, looking around.

"Not in this wood. It was a long time ago, back in the 1960s. People had seen something odd. But that was in the Gaunt Road wood. Not here," said Trevor.

"So, you really think she will be hiding here in some holly bushes?" said Billy, grunting under the exertion of the exercise.

"I don't know for sure. It's as good as place as any," said Trevor.

"If she's not here you can give me back my bus fare," said Spud.

"And mine, eh," said Billy.

"Well, where would you two look then?" said Trevor.

Spud and Billy said nothing. Led by Trevor, the three of them followed the path up into the holly bush section of the wood. There was no wind. All was quiet. The trio trudged on for a few minutes, then Trevor abruptly stopped.

"We're here. This is it," said Trevor, pointing to a clump of holly bushes.

"So, you really think she will be hiding in one of these bushes?" said Spud.

"That's what I reckon," said Trevor.

"You've got to be kidding?" said Spud.

"Looks a waste of time to me. She was a kid when she came here. Things are different when you're grown up," said Billy.

"Yeah, that's right, things are different when you're grown up," said Spud.

Billy and Trevor exchanged glances.

Trevor walked forward and called Amanda's name. Nothing. He called again but there was still nothing. Just bushes and trees looking back at them.

"Stuff this," said Billy, as he stomped over to the bushes and started to look inside the entrances.

The others watched as Billy went from one bush to the other, looking inside before coming out again, frustration written all over his face.

Billy stood and gestured with his arms.

"There's nobody here, it's all empty," said Billy.

Spud kicked the ground.

"I knew it. I knew it. What a waste of time," said Spud.

"Well I thought she would be here," said Trevor, picking up a stick and tossing it aside.

"Hiding in holly bushes? What a mad idea. And we listened to you. Nobody would hide here. As a kid maybe, but not now. I want my bus fare back," said Spud.

"Come on, have another look, we might as well," said Trevor, looking at Billy.

Billy shrugged and went back into the holly bushes. He did the same rounds again. In one bush, out of the other.

"She's definitely not here. There's no trace of anybody being here," said Billy, having now searched every conceivable hiding place among the holly bushes.

"Maybe, maybe there's some more bushes further up?" said Trevor.

Billy walked up the path. After a few minutes, he returned.

"Nah, that's it. Nothing up there, just bare trees," said Billy.

Trevor kicked a loose stone and cursed.

"I really thought she would be here," said Trevor.

"Well, she's not. What a waste of time. What a waste of drinking time. Let's go home. And you, you can pay our bus fare back to Tickhill," said Spud, jabbing a finger at Trevor.

Trevor lingered for a short time, still not convinced that the journey had been a waste of time. Billy came over and patted him on the back.

"Let's go home," said Billy.

Without a word, the three of them made their way down the path, across the stream and over the metal railings.

"Bloody waste of time and effort," said Spud, as they exited the wood.

Then something caught their eye. Three men in black uniforms were dragging a figure up the grassy slope towards a black van that was parked on Ironside Place. The figure, which looked like a girl with blonde hair, was struggling and shouting at the men.

"Shit! That's Amanda!" said Trevor.

Billy took a long look.

"You're right, it is!" said Billy.

"That must be the AFP. They've grabbed her. She was here after all. What do we do?" said Trevor.

"Dunno, but we can't leave her like this, not with those bastards," said Billy.

The three looked at each other. It had been some time since either one of them had done anything violent. Some football hooliganism in their late teens. The odd brick through a window on a drunken night out. But now this, the dreaded AFP manhandling their best mate, Amanda.

Spud stepped forward and clenched his fists.

"I'm up for it, what about you lot?" he said.

Billy and Trevor nodded to Spud.

"Yeah. Let's do it," said Trevor.

"Oh, yeah, let's do it," said Billy.

"What about the Faroe Islands?" said Trevor to Spud.

Spud grimaced.

"Bollocks to the Faroe Islands, they've got Amanda!" shouted Spud.

The three of them started to run. They picked up speed and charged up the slope towards the Anti-Football Police yelling in unison, "Get the bastards!"

Dakerdaker Goes Daft

Boris's brother, Vladimir, had spared no expense to welcome the famous English Super League players, their coaching staff and their glamorous wives and girlfriends. Huge welcoming banners and an array of flags greeted the large ESL contingent as they walked across the tarmac and entered the Dakerdaker airport terminal following their flight from London. Thousands of fans cheered as the entourage wound its way into the reception area of the terminal after passport and immigration formalities. The drugs that many of the players and their wives and girlfriends were carrying were simply ignored.

As the luxury coaches slowly transported them down the Avenue of the Great Vladimir, past the many statues of Vladimir the Great, thousands of fans lined the route waving the flags and banners of the four English Super League clubs. Many chanted the club names and held up huge photographs of the players.

Once ensconced in the luxurious Vladimir the Great Hotel the players gave interviews to the local press. Some players showed their tattoos, while others bragged about how many luxury cars they had and what drugs they used. The wives and girlfriends were also interviewed. Their dresses, make-up and high-heeled shoes being of particular importance to the local journalists.

Lord Milford and Jose Sanchez had arrived earlier in the day and were in the bar at the Vladimir the Great Hotel, a bar that looked like a set from the film *A Clockwork Orange*. Both men were dressed casually. Lord Milford had just observed the circus in the large hotel reception area.

"Well, they're all here. The whole entourage. The whole circus. All we need is a few elephants and a giraffe," said Lord Milford.

"Ah, you are so funny," said Jose Sanchez, finding a comfortable stool at the bar.

Lord Milford shrugged and seated himself next to Jose.

"Well, I managed to persuade the mad lunatic that for this tournament we should play the normal rules," said Lord Milford.

"What is normal anymore?" said Jose.

"Exactly, old chap. What is normal?"

"All I know is that I make money from this football," said Jose, before ordering drinks.

"Yes, but it's not football, is it? Not if Sharkey gets his way. It's insanity," said Lord Milford.

"All life is insanity, amigo. Only time life is sane is when I am making love to a beautiful woman."

Lord Milford welcomed his drink.

"At least our teams make it to the final," said Lord Milford.

"Ah, but who will win?" said Jose, with a grin.

"Never mind the final. Look, what's worrying me is this boat trip to the acid pit of a lake and everyone being vaporised. It's cold-blooded murder. We can't let it happen, old chap."

Jose looked at Lord Milford.

"You know, amigo, I have been thinking hard about this, this boat trip on the lake."

"That's good, good, Jose. And have you come to any conclusions about it?"

"Yes, I have. After much thought, I have decided that we let it happen."

Lord Milford nearly spilled his drink.

"Let it happen?"

"Yes, why not. Provided my two favourite ladies are not on board. As for the rest, I do not care. They are all egos and self-importance on legs."

"So, you, you don't care?"

"No, I do not care. Why should I care? Robot footballers will be better. Less problem, less wages, more money for me."

Lord Milford paused for a few seconds in order to digest Jose's words.

"Right. OK. Good. Right. We let it happen then?" said Lord Milford.

Jose downed his drink in one go.

"Yes, amigo, we let it happen."

The Castle

The fight had been violent but brief. Although Spud, Billy and Trevor had managed to get some good punches in, AFP reinforcements from the black van had overwhelmed them. Tasered and capsicum sprayed, the three of them, along with Amanda, were bungled into the back of the van and whisked away.

In the van, all four of them were trussed up with hand and leg ties and repeatedly clubbed by two sadistic AFP officers. The journey was short, just over an hour, with the van pulling up outside a refurbished castle in the small town of Conisbrough.

The original castle had been built during the reign of William the Conqueror. It was famous for its spectacular keep and it is said that it had inspired Sir Walter Scott to write his novel, Ivanhoe. The government had taken the castle from the National Heritage body and converted it into a detention centre, mainly for dissident football supporters.

The four friends found themselves in a large cell on the ground floor of the keep along with two other females.

"I recognised one of those bastards who hit us. Used to be a Sheffield Wednesday supporter. Always was a dickhead," said Trevor, sitting in a corner.

"What, what are we doing in here?" said Spud, looking around with fear written all over his face.

Amanda sat in another corner. Her face was smeared with dirt and her jeans stained by grass.

"Thanks, guys. Sorry I got you into this mess," said Amanda.

Billy, leaning against a wall, shrugged.

"It's all right, Amanda, we all wanted to have a go at the AFP bastards anyway. It was just a matter of where and when," said Billy.

"He's right. Hey, I really got in a great punch on the fat one. Busted his jaw," said Trevor.

"I got a few good kicks in as well," said Billy, feeling pleased with himself.

Trevor noticed that one of the girls in the cell, the one with red hair, was wearing a Che Guevara badge. Curious, he went over and sat next to her.

"Hey, nice badge," he said.

"Yeah, thanks. My hero," she said.

"Mine too," said Trevor.

At the other end of the cell, Spud was pacing up and down searching for something.

"There's no windows, nothing, we're trapped. Where are we?" said Spud, to the other girl who was slumped in a corner.

The woman in her late twenties was dressed in jeans and a rough jacket. Her hair was pulled up into a tight bun. Her handsome face was slightly bruised.

"Conisbrough Castle. That's where you are. I've been here for about a week. I pissed off the Anti-Football Police by organising a kick-about at my nephew's birthday party for six-year-olds. It was in my back garden. The neighbours dobbed me in. The AFP beat me up. I know I'll be sent to the Faroe Islands, possibly with you lot. Oh, and my name is Anna by the way," she said.

At the mention of the Faroe Islands Spud collapsed against a wall.

"I knew it, I knew it, I knew we'd end up in the Faroe Islands!" shouted Spud.

"Calm down, Spud," said Amanda.

"I'm not going there! No way! It's full of Scots talking gibberish and it's cold and desolate and nobody cares! I can't live on gulls eggs. I have to have my Weetabix every morning!" said Spud, cracking up.

Billy went over and gave Spud a gentle shake.

"Just calm down, Spud. We'll think of something," said Billy.

"He's right, we'll think of something," said Trevor.

"Oh, yeah, think of something! Look where your thinking has got us? Locked up in a castle!" said Spud, throwing himself against the cell door.

Amanda hauled herself to her feet and approached Spud. She was just about to say something when the cell door opened and three AFP officers, one a woman, marched in and grabbed Amanda. They shoved Spud aside and twisted Amanda's arm behind her back and frog marched her out of the cell. Amanda screamed as the door slammed shut.

Let the Games Begin

The Yakadakastan National Stadium, recently re-named The Vladimir the Great Stadium of Truth, Justice, Purity and Enlightenment, was full to capacity in the warm evening sunlight. Almost 80,000 Yakadak football-mad supporters were in the stadium to watch the first semi-final of the Inter-Championship Euro-Asia Cup-Cup between London City FC and Manchester Unity FC.

The format of the tournament was that the two semi-finals would be played consecutively, with the final held the following day. Between the semi-finals and the final, there would be a huge state banquet at the Vladimir the Great Palace in which a giant roast yak would be the piece de resistance.

Seated in the front row of the luxury seating in the VIP section of the main stand was Hank Sharkey, in his best Armani suit, and Zaza in a tight-fitting, low-cut gold dress. Next to Zaza was Boris in a strange bottle green military uniform and his brother Vladimir on an imperial throne. Vladimir was dressed in a bright red military uniform complete with rows of medals and large epaulettes. Behind them sat Lord Milford and Jose Sanchez and behind them was a blow-up, look-a-like replica of Tony Campbell. The real

Tony Campbell was back in his hotel room dazed and battered by a colossal hangover.

"Should be a good game," said Boris, looking at Zaza but talking to Sharkey.

"Oh, yeah, would be better if we were playing to the new rules," said Sharkey.

The beginning of the tournament was signalled by the playing of the Yakadakastan national anthem. This was played over the ubiquitous loudspeakers to the tune of Paul McCartney's Mull of Kintyre, with the repetitive words Oh, Vladimir the Great substituted for the original lyrics.

Finally, the teams walked out on to the pitch accompanied by a cacophony of sound. London City FC in red, Manchester Unity FC in blue. The players lined up either side of the match officials who were all dressed in pink. After the players had saluted and genuflected to Vladimir the match got underway.

The start of the game was a tight affair with neither side wanting to commit any early errors. For the first fifteen minutes no team could manage a shot at goal or even force a corner. The play drifted aimlessly until the referee inexplicably gave London City FC a penalty despite the play and ball being well inside the London City FC half of the field.

"What the hell was that for?" said Lord Milford, clearly agitated.

Hank Sharkey yawned. He had no idea either, but it was for his team so he didn't care.

"Relax, Lord Baby. You'll win the game, remember?" said Sharkey, nodding.

Zaza stroked Sharkey's forehead, then kissed him.

After some fruitless arguing by the Manchester Unity FC players, Methuselah Jackson calmly strolled up and scored from the penalty kick putting London City FC 1-0 up. But before Manchester Unity FC could re-start the game the referee blew his whistle for half-time.

"He's blown far too early," said Lord Milford, jumping to his feet.

"At least fifteen more minutes to go by my watch," said Jose, checking his watch, just to be sure.

Boris also jumped to his feet.

"Excuse myself, I have to go and make love to one of my mistresses," he said, before disappearing down a back stairwell.

From another stairwell, a man in uniform appeared and nervously approached Vladimir before grovelling at his feet. He mumbled something to the Great Leader, averting his eyes and bobbing his head as he relayed the information. Vladimir shrugged, then snarled, "Kill them all!"

The man mumbled something, nodded, stood, saluted and exited without further delay. Vladimir turned to Sharkey and Zaza.

"I have just been informed by that idiot that workers at my baked bean factories want a pay rise and shorter working hours. I ask you, one dollar a day for working a fourteen-hour day is fair. Am I not a just and fair man?" said Vladimir.

"Perfectly fair, Your Greatness. Workers expect far too much these days," said Sharkey.

"You are a very generous man," said Zaza, leaning over and touching Vladimir affectionately on the shoulder.

"Indeed I am. Why, why is such a great man as myself bothered by these trivialities, why?" said Vladimir, clearly exasperated.

Behind them, Lord Milford had now settled down and was eating a cucumber sandwich. Jose was also preoccupied playing a game on his phone.

The sun went behind the clouds and a great shadow covered the stadium. A small military band marched out on to the pitch and played a juddering jumble of seemingly out-of-tune marching music. Slowly the crowd filtered back into the stadium after the half-time refreshments. Finally, a great roar greeted the players as they jogged out for the second half. Boris also returned, zipping up his fly, as he seated himself next to Zaza.

The game kicked off again to the accompaniment of cheering from the crowd. Manchester Unity FC came forward in numbers looking for the equaliser but London City FC defended well, clearing the danger. Then, with the ball on the half-way line, the referee again, inexplicably, awarded London City FC a penalty.

"What the hell was that for?" yelled Lord Milford, climbing to his feet.

"Relax, Lord Baby, remember the deal. Your team wins," said Sharkey.

As an angry Lord Milford seated himself, Methuselah Jackson slammed home his second penalty kick of the game. The score was now 2-0 to London City FC.

Manchester Unity FC made a few substitutions and attacked down both wings. The London City FC defence was put under great pressure. Finally, the speedy Manchester Unity FC forward, Bobby Duffield, broke through into the

London City FC penalty area, only to be hacked down and stomped on by the London City FC centre back, the notorious Silvio Battersby.

"It's got to be a penalty!" shouted Lord Milford, jumping to his feet. Hank Sharkey looked at him then yawned.

Much to Lord Milford's obvious frustration, the referee waved play on. A speechless Lord Milford collapsed into his seat gasping for breath.

From there on play got bogged down in mid-field duals with plenty of petty fouls and irrelevant throw-ins. There was also lots of time-wasting by London City FC players as they rolled around on the ground every time a Manchester Unity FC player breathed on them.

Up in the stands Sharkey had fallen asleep, while Boris had his hand on Zaza's thigh. Jose had gone to the toilet, returned, gone to the toilet and returned, while Vladimir continued to polish the medals on his chest. Meanwhile, Lord Milford was becoming more agitated. Sweat poured down his face as he kept looking at his watch.

As Lord Milford checked his watch for the umpteenth time, a strong gust of wind lifted up the blow-up replica of Tony Campbell and blew it on to the pitch and into the Manchester Unity FC penalty area as London City FC launched an attack. A defender, moving quickly, tried to hack the ball clear but the ball hit the blow-up Tony Campbell and bounced back into the Manchester Unity FC net. The referee had no hesitation in awarding a goal. The score was now 3-0 to London City FC.

"For heavens' sake! You can't give that!" yelled Lord Milford.

As the players lined up to restart the game the referee blew his whistle for full time. The players dutifully trooped off the field without a word of protest. Up in the VIP area, Lord Milford stood and began to wave his hands about in sheer frustration.

"You've blown up twenty minutes early! You fool, you idiot! We've been robbed!" he shouted.

But nobody was listening. Sharkey was fast asleep, Boris and Zaza were kissing passionately, Vladimir was still polishing his medals and Jose was on the toilet.

Room 102

From Conisbrough Castle, Amanda had been taken in a black van to an office block in a town that she didn't recognise. She was allocated a room with a bed, washbasin and toilet facilities. Amanda did her best to clean herself up, washing her face and attempting to rub out the grass stains on her blue jeans and pink jumper. She combed her long hair and pulled it into a ponytail. After that effort, she collapsed on the bed and slipped into a deep sleep.

Sometime later she was awakened by a muscular Anti-Football Police officer jabbing her hard on the upper arm. Without a word, the officer pulled her to her feet and dragged her from the room. Amanda was forcibly taken up a flight of stairs and into a small, windowless room that was occupied by a table and two chairs. It was similar to the rooms she had seen in countless TV cop shows; the room where the cops interrogate the suspects. The AFP officer then left, locking the door behind him. Amanda wearily sat at the table and wondered what would happen next.

Amanda wasn't kept waiting. After ten minutes, two AFP officers entered the room. The broad-shouldered, crop-haired male officer stood by the door, while the smaller female officer seated herself opposite Amanda. The woman was youngish with short black hair. She wore bright red lipstick and a tight-fitting open-neck black AFP uniform. She placed some sheets of paper and a pen in front of her on the table, cleared her throat and looked firmly at Amanda. The two women looked at each other for longer than seemed normal.

"You are Amanda Harper? Yes?" said the AFP officer, eventually.

"Yes. I am."

"You are unemployed, but before that, you were a library assistant, yes?"

"Yes. Before the council closed the library."

"You live at Tickhill in a flat on Tithes Lane. Number 8 in a block of 16. Is that correct?"

"Yes."

The AFP officer scribbled on the paper in front of her. Amanda noticed that the woman had beautifully manicured fingernails.

"Now, two days ago, you sent out messages and texts to countless social media sites. Is this true?"

The AFP had Amanda's laptop and phone so it was no use denying things.

"Yes, it's true."

The interrogator placed her elbows on the table and leaned forward. The next sentence she articulated very carefully.

"The message that you sent was a false news message stating that the English Super League stadiums were infected by a killer flu. Is this correct?"

Amanda paused. She thought she would let the clever bitch wait for the answer. The two women stared at each other. Fifteen seconds passed.

"I said, is this correct?"

Amanda glared at the AFP officer. Despite the situation, Amanda liked the look of her face.

"Yes. It's correct."

"Good."

The AFP officer scribbled all this information furiously on to the paper in front of her.

"So, you admit to doing this?"

Amanda didn't answer.

"I said, do you admit to doing this?"

"Yes. I do."

The woman leaned back in her chair.

"Good, that makes our job a lot easier."

The AFP officer leaned forward and wrote furiously again on the paper. The male officer by the door looked on impassively. The woman then thrust the paper and a pen at Amanda.

"Sign at the bottom."

Amanda pulled the paper closer to her and glanced at it.

"Why? What am I signing?"

"That is a statement of admission that you sent out false news on social media to disrupt English Super League games. Sign it at the bottom."

Slowly Amanda picked up the pen. She looked at the document, but could not read the scribble that supposedly passed for handwriting. After fifteen seconds or so of useless scrutiny, she signed the document. Immediately the woman snatched the sheet back and inspected Amanda's signature. Satisfied, she stood and made for the door.

"What happens now? Do I get sent to the Faroe Islands?" said Amanda.

The woman stopped, turned, put one hand on her hip and gave Amanda a hard stare.

"No. Nothing so comfortable. Soon you will be executed. Hung, drawn and then quarted. You will be decapitated and your pretty head will be put on display in a public place for all to see for some time to come as an example. That is a pity. In another life, you and I could perhaps have been close friends, maybe even lovers. Enjoy the rest of your day."

Amanda stared at the AFP officer open-mouthed.

The woman winked at Amanda, mouthed a kiss and gave a faint hint of a smile. The two AFP officers turned and exited, locking the door and leaving Amanda alone to contemplate the fate that seemingly awaited her.

The Games Continue

As night shadows cloaked the stadium the powerful floodlights were turned on. The crowd gave a big cheer as it was the first time they had seen lights on at night since Vladimir the Great had come to power. The only lights permitted after dark were in the Vladimir the Great Palace, which was lit up every night like a giant Christmas tree.

Up in the VIP area of the stand, Hank Sharkey and Zaza were missing, as was Vladimir. They had moved on to the Vladimir the Great Palace in preparation for the state banquet later that evening. Boris and Jose Sanchez were still there, keen to watch how their teams would perform. Lord Milford was also still in the stadium. He was slumped in his chair behind Boris and Jose, talking to himself, but afraid to confront Sharkey over the result of the first semi-final.

The teams finally came out of the tunnel, with the same referee leading the officials. The crowd roared as Birmingham Villa FC in blue and Merseyside FC in red warmed up by jogging on the spot. As Vladimir was not in the stadium the national anthem was not relayed over the loudspeakers. Instead, Elton John's Crocodile Rock thundered out followed by George Ezra's Paradise. The crowd roared their approval and began to sing along to the songs.

Back on the field, Birmingham Villa FC was about to kick-off when a herd of wild goats wandered on to the pitch. The goats started to graze in the Merseyside FC penalty area. This delayed the kick-off for ten minutes until they were all shot by security guards. There were more delays as the carcases were picked up and tossed into a skip and set alight. Finally, with the rock music playing and the crowd still singing madly, Birmingham Villa FC kicked off and the second semi-final finally got underway.

Jose was curious about the identity of the referee, the same man who had given the strange decisions in the first semi-final. He leaned closer to Boris.

"Who is the referee, Boris, amigo?" said Jose.

Boris chuckled.

"He is my brother, Igor Igoravitch. He is very fair. A good man."

Jose turned to look at Lord Milford, then sank into his seat and held his head.

However, the game was a fairly even affair, with both sets of players aware of each other's capabilities. Surprisingly, the referee refereed very well. He gave sensible free kicks to each team and was scrupulous in awarding correct goal kicks, throw-ins and corner kicks. The supporters cheered wildly as the game spluttered to a 0-0 half-time score-line.

As the half-time whistle sounded, Boris disappeared again down the same stairwell. Jose turned to Lord Milford.

"So, far so good, amigo. The referee is very fair. I cannot fault him," said Jose, smiling.

"Yes, but the game is not over yet, Jose," said Lord Milford.

Jose's smile disappeared from his handsome face.

During the interval, an over-excited fan ran on to the pitch waving a red and white scarf. He was immediately shot by security guards and his body dragged from the pitch and dumped in the skip. The crowd roared with delight.

"So that's how they deal with pitch invasions here," said Lord Milford, shaking his head.

Jose stared in disbelief.

The band came on to the pitch again and played a medley of unrecognisable marching tunes. Then Boris returned, zipping his fly before sitting. The band finally marched off playing a cacophony of music as the players returned for the second half.

Merseyside FC did most of the attacking from the kick-off but couldn't break down a tough Birmingham Villa FC defence. The game went deep into the second half with few incidents until the floodlights mysteriously went out. The stadium was plunged into darkness.

The lights were only off for a moment but when they came back on again the ball was in the back of the Merseyside FC net and the referee was pointing to the centre spot. He had just given a goal to Birmingham Villa FC.

Jose was speechless. Boris jumped up and cheered.

"Yes! A brilliant goal!" shouted Boris.

Lord Milford leaned forward and tapped Jose on the shoulder.

"Hard luck, old boy. I bet the next thing to happen will be the full-time whistle."

Several Merseyside FC players complained to the referee, but he refused to listen to their pleas. The disgruntled players lined up for the kick-off just as the full-time whistle blew. Birmingham Villa FC had won, 1-0.

"Ah, only ten minutes too soon this time," said Lord Milford, looking at his watch.

It was only then that Lord Milford noticed a small envelope on his seat, an envelope that must have been placed there during the blackout. Lord Milford opened it. He read the message carefully and handed it to Jose Sanchez. Jose read the letter. The two exchanged concerned glances and immediately departed the stadium.

All Alone

After the interrogation, Amanda had been escorted back to her small cell. She had asked the escorting male AFP officer if she could speak to the female officer again, but he ignored her. She asked him if she had any legal rights but the officer had turned his back and locked the door behind him. Amanda, tired and dejected, slumped on to the bed and fell asleep.

About an hour later Amanda woke suddenly from a disturbing slumber. In a dream, she had been playing football for Grimsby Town. But the goals had been the holly bushes from the wood and the goalkeeper was a giant custard tart. In her black and white striped shirt and black shorts, Amanda had dribbled around a huge laptop and scored a goal by shooting a loaf of bread into the holly bush entrance. She had run around the pitch in triumph, celebrating the goal, only to be pulled aside by the female AFP officer from the interrogation and smothered in hot, wet kisses. That was when Amanda woke up.

With the dream still all too fresh in her mind, Amanda washed her face in the sink in a vain attempt to rid herself of the dream's goal celebration. After that, she slumped reluctantly back on to the bed and stared at the ceiling. The nightmare made her wary of ever falling asleep again.

She thought about the AFP officer's chilling words. 'Hung, drawn and quartered.' Hadn't Mel Gibson been hung, drawn and quartered in that Scottish rebellion film she had seen some years ago on late-night TV? At school, she had been taught that those who had tried to blow up the Houses of Parliament, way back in the early 1600s, had all been hung drawn and quartered. Amanda shuddered.

Frustrated and bored, she looked around the room for something to occupy her mind. On the table near the bed was a yellowing *Tiger* comic that had somehow survived being tossed away. Reluctantly, Amanda reached out and picked it up. She lazily flipped the pages.

The Roy of the Rovers story in the middle pages caught her attention for a short period. In the story, Roy, who was normally a gun centre forward, was somehow playing in goal for Melchester Rovers in a big European final. With the score at 1-1, the opposition was awarded a penalty in the dying minutes of the game. Roy dived one way as the shot went to other. Turning over the page, Amanda was surprised to see Roy had saved the penalty by anticipating the banana-like swerve on the ball. Not only that, Roy plonked the ball down on the floor and dribbled the whole opposition team to score at the other end. The crowd had just witnessed the greatest goal ever scored in a football game. But a voice bubble from the crowd said, "About time, Roy, you left that a bit late!" Amanda tossed the comic aside.

So, what was to be done? Amanda couldn't think properly. Her mind was a jumble of mixed thoughts. One minute she had been buying groceries, the next she was confined in a cell. She had no idea where she was or what to do, or if she was entitled to any legal advice. Everything had happened so quickly and all over football. Bloody football!

She stretched her legs against the metal bar at the end of the bed and thought of her childhood. She thought of life with her mum and childhood holidays in places like Skegness, Scarborough, Blackpool and Great Yarmouth. Then, as an adult, her first trip to Spain, the drug scene in Portugal and getting sloshed with mates on the Greek Islands. She thought about her first serious boyfriend, Jed. What was he doing now? Then her mind wandered to the various jobs she had done and then on to her relationship with dumb, but handsome Spud.

The thoughts were all too much for her. Amanda punched the pillow in frustration. She closed her eyes as a tear slid down her freckled cheek.

Apocalypse Now!

The huge tapestry decorated banquet hall in the Vladimir the Great Palace was rapidly filling with guests. On a raised platform at the top end of the hall Vladimir Igoravitch, Supreme Ruler of Yakadakastan, was seated on a diamond-encrusted throne beneath the huge crest of an eagle. For this special occasion, Vladimir was dressed in a white uniform festooned with medals. He was also wearing what looked like a busby. Next to him was his attractive, long-time mistress, Olga, in an elegant, tight-fitting blue dress. Beside her was Boris. He was wearing a navy-blue uniform and hat that made him look like a 1960s bus conductor. Seated next to Boris was Zaza in a long, low-cut red dress. Beside her sat Hank Sharkey, well encased in a blue, herring-bone suit. There was also seating for Jose Sanchez, Lord Milford and the British Prime Minister Tony Campbell, but, strangely, none of them were present.

The other guests were prominent ministers in the government, Boris's many female escorts and a platoon of black-uniformed security guards, all well-armed with Kalashnikovs, swords and pistols, but all looking worse for wear following some heavy drinking during the semi-finals.

After some traditional dancing by local girls and a performance by an acrobat troop, Vladimir felt hungry enough to dispense with any further pre-dinner entertainment. He impatiently dismissed a magician, clapped his hands and demanded that the meal commence. Seconds after his command the great doors to the banquet hall swung open and a large roasted yak was wheeled into the hall on an equally large gurney by a platoon of kitchen hands. A pineapple was jammed in the yak's mouth, while fruit and meat cuts were laid out along the body length of the roasted animal.

"What a magnificent animal. It will make a splendid meal," said Vladimir, salivating.

"It looks delicious," said Boris.

Hank Sharkey wasn't sure what to make of it all.

"Yeah, looks kinda great, Your Supreme Highness," said Sharkey.

"Now, you idiots, prepare our food," said Vladimir, shouting and gesticulating at the kitchen hands.

The kitchen hands produced large knives and forks and began to slice chunks of meat from the yak and place it on plates. The plates were then hurriedly placed in front of the guests. This was followed by more kitchen staff spooning vegetables from large saucepans on to all the plates over the shoulders of the guests. However, nobody dared commence eating until Vladimir had given the order. After seeing his own plate piled high with food Vladimir waved the kitchen hands away and gave the command to eat.

"Everyone eat. Everyone enjoy! And you, you kitchen scum, get out of my banquet hall, now!" shouted Vladimir.

The kitchen hands bowed and obsequiously exited the banquet hall.

As Vladimir gave the order, Zaza stood and whispered to Sharkey.

"Excuse me, I think I have the beginnings of the Yakadak Runs. I must go to the toilet at once, darling," she said.

"Ah, that's OK, baby, I understand. I had a bit of tummy trouble this morning. But I'm fine now, baby. Don't be long. You know I love having you seated beside me," said Sharkey, winking.

Zaza blew Sharkey a kiss, bowed to Vladimir and exited the banquet hall. Once out of the hall Zaza took off her stiletto heels, tossed them aside and ran as best she could down a short, but winding staircase and out of the front doors of the palace.

She ran down the long driveway, ignoring bemused guards, and continued through the tall gates. She ran towards the white-coated kitchen hands that were now assembled, beneath a grove of trees in a small park opposite the palace.

Once there, Zaza, totally breathless, immediately slumped into the arms of a tall, bearded man who was wearing a stained kitchen-hand uniform. The two kissed with enthusiasm and passion. Seconds later the Vladimir the Great Palace disintegrated, blown to pieces by a massive explosion.

Akerdaker in Dakerdaker

Within hours of the explosion in Dakerdaker, the world's media were on the scene. Standing in front of the still smouldering ruins of the Vladimir the Great Palace, Cloud News's ace reporter Jason Incredible, wearing a combat shirt complete with dog tags, was preparing to do a piece-to-camera. Behind him were scenes of wild jubilation as happy Yakadakastani's danced for joy, pulled down statues and burned effigies and photographs of Vladimir Igoravitch. Accompanying this mayhem were hits by AC/ DC thumping out of the ubiquitous street loudspeakers.

"What amazing scenes. The people are going crazy. Here I am, Jason Incredible, standing here in front of the ruins of the Vladimir the Great Palace that was blown to a smouldering ruin only hours ago. It is rumoured the bomb was placed inside a roast yak that was to be served to the President and his guests. What we do know is that the President, Vladimir the Great, is dead along with his brother Boris Igoravitch. Also dead is Vladimir's mistress, Olga and the President of the English Super League, Hank Sharkey. Credit for the assassination has been attributed to the Yakadakastan People's Liberation Popular Front lead by Fidel Guevara Smith, brother of the late Che Castro Smith. Fidel is here, with me now. Would you like to say a few words to the world, Fidel?"

Fidel Guevara Smith, standing off-camera, moved into camera shot as Jason thrust the microphone beneath his bushy beard. Fidel, still in his kitchen-hand costume, stared straight at the camera.

"The tyrant and his brother tyrant are finally dead. The tyrant who plotted to kill my brother is dead. The tyrant's brother who was also the tyrant who killed my brother, is dead. I am proud I killed the tyrant and his brother, who also was a tyrant because he killed my brother, who was not a tyrant. Now Yakadakastan is free of tyrants," shouted Fidel, pumping his clenched fist.

The camera moved back to Jason who was not quite sure what to make of Fidel's rant.

"Tell me, was the bomb inside the yak, Fidel?" said Jason.

"Yes. Boom! Boom! What a beautiful explosion. It was a brilliant idea of my girlfriend, Zaza. She is very clever," said Fidel, all pumped up.

"And Zaza is the girl in the red dress, standing next to you?" said Jason.

"Yes, you speak to her now," said Fidel.

Zaza came into shot still wearing the low-cut red dress.

"Zaza, I understand it was your idea to put the bomb in the yak?" said Jason, his eyes glued to Zaza's cleavage.

"Yes. I am so proud of this moment. Bomb in yak, boom! I would just like to say, firstly, we have liberated Yakadakastan from a tyrant. Secondly, the world is also rid of the dreadful Hank Sharkey. I hated him."

"Why was that?" said Jason.

"Because I am part Venezuelan and part Osage Indian. Many years ago, Sharkey's relatives killed my relatives to get the oil that was beneath land granted to us by the United States Government. It made him very rich. I first learned of this when, not long ago, I met Fidel Smith at Havana University. We became lovers, hot lovers and he told me of this great injustice. Today was sweet revenge. I have also saved all the footballers in this tournament. They were all to die on the acid lake just outside of the city. But fortunately, they are all going home safe, including the owners of the other English Super League clubs. Also, your Prime Minster is safe. I slipped him a Mickey Finn on the flight over here to make him ill so he would miss the banquet. It saved his life," said Zaza.

Jason Incredible, who knew nothing about this, nothing of recent Yakadakastan history and nothing about anything, pretended he did.

"Yes, I understand. Well done. If I could just get Fidel back into the picture," said Jason.

Fidel, smiling like a ten-year-old, moved back into camera shot and stood next to Zaza.

"Fidel, I understand you will be the next President of Yakadakastan?" said Jason.

"Yes, I will be the next president. I democratically killed my way to power," said Fidel, with great pride.

"Yes, I see. Could you tell the world your future plans for the people of Yakadakastan?" said Jason.

"My people are now free. A tyrant is dead. You see how happy they are?" said Fidel, as behind him a group of youths trashed a supermarket.

"So, what are your future plans for your country, Fidel?" said Jason, keen to wind things up.

"My future plans? Firstly, today is a day of celebration. They are happy. So happy. Secondly, my own tyranny will commence tomorrow," said Fidel.

"Congratulations, to you both, Fidel and Zaza," said Jason, as though Fidel and Zaza were a couple who had just won a dance contest. Jason then turned to the camera.

"This is Jason Incredible, reporting from Dakerdaker, Yakerdakerstan for Cloud News."

Breaking News

Following the reports of the violent events in Dakerdaker, the media excitedly reported a volcanic eruption in the south of Iceland, a jet crash and a sudden death at Heathrow Airport. Again, Cloud News was the first with this 'Breaking News.'

"In further breaking news, the Laki volcano in southern Iceland erupted unexpectedly today. The volcano, that has not erupted since 1784, spewed huge amounts of ash and debris into the atmosphere. Fishermen on a trawler said that they saw an out-of-control small jet disappear into the mouth of the volcano at about the same time as the eruption. Experts believe that the jet sucked up ash and debris into the planes' engines causing it to crash. According to air traffic control in Reykjavik, the plane carried Icelandic national Jose Sanchez, the online betting tycoon and owner of Merseyside FC. The odds on the Laki volcano erupting were 43 to 1," said Jocelyn Radish-Hamster, Cloud News's top anchor-woman.

"And, in further bad news for the English Super League, Lord Milford, owner of Manchester Unity FC, dropped dead today as he disembarked from his own Lear Jet which had just landed from Dakerdaker. Lord Milford told a ground steward that he felt unwell as he disembarked, but he then collapsed headfirst into a waste paper bin as he entered the VIP lounge at Heathrow Airport. Lord Milford was rushed to hospital but was pronounced dead on arrival. He was 74. And now, golf..."

Billy had managed to pick up this television broadcast online, live, on his second phone, including a text relaying the news from Yakadakastan. An excited and agitated Billy looked across the cell in Conisbrough Castle at the others. Spud was asleep cuddled up close to Anna, while Trevor and Jenner, the girl with the Che Guevara badge, were engaged in frenetic kissing.

Billy went over to them, gesticulating wildly.

"Hey, you lot, wake up! Wake up! I've got something important to tell y'," said Billy.

Slowly, the others gave him some attention.

"What?" said Trevor, annoyed that his snog with Jenner had been interrupted.

"Yeah, what," said Spud, giving Billy unenthusiastic attention.

Billy relayed to them the information about the deaths in Dakerdaker, the volcanic explosion, the crashed Lear Jet that contained Jose Sanchez and the sudden death of Lord Milford. It took a little time for the news to sink in.

"Are you sure?" said Anna, getting to her feet.

"It's on my second phone. I hid it in a secret pocket. It's true! The ratbags are all dead," said Billy, holding up his phone.

"What, you've just heard it?" said Spud.

"Yeah! They're all dead! Including Sharkey. Blown up in Yakadakerstan. There was a coup there," said Billy.

"What's a coup?" said Spud.

"A coup, it's a... never mind. Bloody hell! If that's true! it means, it means..." said Trevor, not sure to believe that it was all true and what it meant.

"It means what?" said Spud, standing open-mouthed.

"It means, well, don't you see. If Sharkey, Sanchez and Lord Milford and that Boris bastard are all dead, then football is not dead, real football that is. Football can live again! It's Sharkey's billions that keep it all going. If he's dead, then the English Super League is possibly finished," said Billy.

"Then, then football as we knew it can start again? Is that what you're saying?" said Spud, looking shell shocked.

"It is true isn't it? You're not playing games with us," said Trevor, confronting Billy.

"Honest. Here, I'll show y'," said Billy, pulling out his phone.

Trevor took advantage of the pause to give Jenner another big kiss.

"Hang on, there's something else coming through," said Billy as he looked at his phone.

"What?" said Spud, as he held Anna close.

"Bloody hell. A text. More Breaking News. It says that the prime minister, Tony Campbell, who is believed to be suffering from a massive hangover in a Dakerdaker hotel room, has been removed in a vote of no confidence in the House of Commons and that Peter Corbett is now the new prime minister," said Billy, excitedly.

For a second everyone was open-mouthed.

"Corbett? Peter Corbett the new prime minister? Hey, he's all right, Corbett. He's the only politician who voted against this English Super League shit!" said Trevor.

"Yeah, listen, Corbett has made an announcement. Corbett says that the ESL will be no more, it will be disbanded and that the Anti-Football Police will also be disbanded, immediately, and that football will return to normal!" said Billy, reading from his phone.

"Give me that," said Trevor, snatching Billy's phone.

Trevor read the online article, mouthing the words as he worked his way through the text.

"It's true! Yes! Viva the Revolution!" shouted Trevor, before kissing Jenner again.

"Yes!" shouted, Billy, pumping a fist in the air.

But Spud was having none of it.

"Hang on. It's crap! I don't believe it. Not one word of it. It's all too good to be true. I bet it's all a joke, a laugh, false news to bring out into the open those who oppose the ESL. It's all a lie. We're all going to be sent to the Faroe Islands. I know it! I bet you're making it all up, you bastard. We're still imprisoned in here aren't we?" said Spud, making a wild gesture with his hands.

But just as Spud finished speaking the cell door slowly opened wide, seemingly by itself, and stayed open.

Reunion

The old friends were back together again, seated around their favourite table in the Royal Oak, pint glasses of beer and soggy crisps in front of them. Amanda told Spud, Trevor and Billy about what happened after she was taken from the cell in the castle, while the lads gave detailed versions of their time in the cell.

Billy was delighted to mention that he and Molly, his barmaid girlfriend from Barnsley, were back together again following some romantic texting. Trevor was also eager to tell Amanda that he had found his true soul mate in Jenner, a fellow Marxist-Leninist-Trotskyite-Maoist. But Spud, well Spud, was a little reluctant to let Amanda know that he and Anna were now an item.

"After just a few hours and a kiss and a cuddle in a damp cell, you're going steady?" said Billy.

"Oh, yeah. We're talking of pets, kids and mortgages and school fees," said Spud, excitedly.

"All that costs money and you haven't got a job yet, Spud," said Trevor.

Spud scratched his head.

"Oh, yeah, I never thought of that," said Spud.

Amanda reached out and touched Spud's hand.

"It's all right, Spud. You dream and I hope you and Anna will be very happy together," said Amanda.

"No hard feelings, then?" said Spud, dipping his head.

"No, no hard feelings at all, Spud," said Amanda.

After a few jokes and a laugh about the fake flu epidemic and the fight outside the wood with the Anti-Football Police, the talk turned invariably to football.

"It's looking good. Real good. With all the mega-owners dead, Corbett has announced that the English Super League is no more. None of the next-of-kin of the mega-owners has voiced any interest in taking over the clubs. So, Corbett says that the four ESL clubs are to disband immediately. They're finished!" said Billy, downing his pint.

"Yeah, great, but what I saw this morning on Cloud News is that the first sixteen clubs that can prove that they are financially viable and can produce a safe home ground, will be allowed to become members of the New Premier League," said Trevor.

"Yeah, sounds good, but you know who that will be?" said Billy.

"Yeah, don't I know it. The same suspects. Liverpool, Man City, Man U, Arsenal, Chelsea and Spurs. They have the money, we don't. Once they disentangle themselves from the defunct ESL clubs, they'll be back just as before and our little clubs will be back to square one again, in League One or Two or even worse," said Trevor.

"What's worse?" said Spud.

"Playing in the Faroe Islands Premier League!" said Trevor.

"I'm not going up there!" said Spud, still traumatised by the very words, Faroe Islands.

"It's a joke, Spud," said Amanda, laughing.

"Hey, what about all the players from the ESL?" said Billy.

"That bunch of useless scum. Mercenaries, the lot of 'em. Most of them have gone to clubs in the Mongolian Premier League. Good riddance to the lot of 'em," said Trevor.

"Yeah, they can all piss off!" said Spud.

Everybody took a drink of their beer.

"Corbett says that he hopes the New Premier League and the rest of the football league will be up and running by August," said Billy.

Just then, two well-dressed men, with sharp haircuts and carrying briefcases, entered the Royal Oak. They had a quick word with a barman before making their way towards Billy, Spud, Trevor and Amanda. One of the men, the older man wearing a dark grey suit, approached Amanda.

"Excuse me, but are you Amanda Harper?"

Amanda flicked her blonde hair back and looked quizzically at the two men.

"Yes, that's me, who wants to know?"

"My name is Paget, Steven Paget, and I represent a firm of solicitors, Black, Green and Gold. We have just arrived from London. May we have a word with you on a very important matter? Oh, and this is my colleague, Andrew Taylor."

Taylor smiled and nodded. Nobody acknowledged him.

Amanda shot looks at her mates and then turned to Paget.

"How did you know I was here?" said Amanda.

"Ah, yes. We went to your address and a neighbour said that you would probably be here. She gave a good description of you as well," said Paget.

"That will be Deidre. Did she have her hair in curlers?" said Amanda, looking at Paget.

"Yes, she did. Now if you wouldn't..."

"What's this all about then?" said Amanda, cutting him off.

"I'm glad you asked that question. It is a very private matter. Very delicate. Could we have a quite word, please. Perhaps there is somewhere we can go?" said Paget, looking around.

"Can't you say what you have to say in front of my mates?" said Amanda.

"Ah, I'm afraid not. This is important and private business. Please, I assure you we will be brief," said Paget.

Amanda hesitated. She looked at her mates, then at the two men.

"All right, if you insist. There's a nice cafe across the road, we can go there."

"Splendid, lead the way," said Paget, nodding to the lads.

Amanda stood and addressed her mates.

"Won't be long."

Amanda, Paget and Taylor exited the Royal Oak and made their way across the road to the Boulevard Cafe as Trevor, Billy and Spud all looked at each other in amusement and some bewilderment.

Big Business

In the Boulevard Cafe the three of them seated themselves in a private section towards the rear. The cafe was warm and comfortable with well-upholstered chairs. Prints of Edward Hopper paintings were spaced thoughtfully on cream-coloured walls. Paget ordered three coffees from the waitress while Taylor pulled papers from the worn briefcase that he was carrying.

"Have you lived here long?" said Paget, smiling.

"Most of my life, why?" said Amanda.

"Nothing, it's just..."

"Will you say what you have to say and then bugger off. I'm getting a little fed up of this posh talk crap and you two not saying anything specific, although I suppose that's what solicitors are trained to do," said Amanda.

The waitress brought the coffees and diplomatically retreated.

"Very well, Ms Harper. I'll be brief and I will do as you ask. Now, did you know that your mother spent some time employed as a waitress in London?" said Paget.

"My mother? Yes, I know that. It was before I was born. She told me about it. So what?"

"Well, she worked for a time at Claridge's Hotel in Mayfair. A very up-market establishment. While she was there, she also met some interesting individuals. One of whom was a Lord Milford. Do you recognise that name?"

Amanda was taken aback for a moment.

"What, Lord Milford the owner, well, the late owner of Manchester Unity FC?"

"Yes, indeed. The very same Lord Milford. Who sadly is now deceased. Well apparently, your mother and Lord Milford, how shall I say this, your mother and Lord Milford co-habited together."

Amanda looked at Taylor then back at Paget.

"What? You mean, you mean, they had sex?"

"Yes. Sex."

"My mother and Lord Milford?"

"Yes. Your mother and Lord Milford. And you, Amanda, you, are the product of that sex."

"Me?"

"Yes, you."

"What? You're saying that, that Lord Milford is, was my dad?"

"Yes, it seems so. Lord Milford was your father."

Amanda was not quite sure what to say to this. All she could feel was a lump inside her stomach and a tightening in her throat.

"Are you sure? This is not a joke is it, because if it is..."

"I assure you Amanda, it is no joke."

"You're sure about this?"

"Yes. Positive. Otherwise we would not be here wasting our time," said Paget.

"But why didn't Lord Milford try to contact me if he knew I was his daughter?"

"Only he would know that, Amanda," said Paget.

Amanda leaned back in her chair. Paget had a point. If this was crap it was a long way to come to play a stupid prank.

"Yeah, well, mum never said. She never said. All these years. She must have kept it all bottled up. She only said that dad had run off before I was born. When I asked when I got older, she said that she had no idea where he was and refused to talk about him. There was nothing said about a bloody Lord Milford."

Paget took a sip of his coffee before replying.

"Sometimes, people have trouble revealing their past, Amanda. There is often nothing sinister in this. It's just that they would rather forget the past and move on."

"Yeah, maybe," said Amanda.

"It's all true, Amanda. Milford, of course, knew all along. He knew all about you. I can only speculate that he may have helped your mother financially from time to time. I know your mother kept in touch with him. The last time was before she died about, what, four years ago?"

"Yeah, breast cancer. Not nice."

"Yes, I'm sorry, Amanda. Anyway. Can you see where this is going?"

"Going? I'm not sure if I'm coming yet. It's all a bit of a shock."

"You don't want to leave and re-join your mates across the road?" said Taylor, with a touch of sarcasm.

"Just get on with what you have to say," snapped Amanda, momentarily back to her old self.

Paget gave Taylor a withering look. He then put both his hands together on the table and gave Amanda his well-practised avuncular look.

"Very well, Amanda. I shall explain. Putting it succinctly, Lord Milford had no other direct or living relatives. None whatsoever. His marriage was childless and his wife died some years ago. You, Amanda Harper, are the sole beneficiary of Lord Milford's estate. You are his acknowledged daughter, his only direct living relative, and, as a result, you have been bequeathed quite a substantial amount of money and property. Quite a substantial amount. There are taxes to pay, inheritance tax, a few debts and such, but all in all you will be left with a very large sum of money totalling..."

On cue, Taylor slipped a piece of paper in front of Amanda with a financial amount boldly written on it.

"Shit!" said Amanda, glaring at the figure.

"Indeed. A very, very, big pile of shit," said Paget.

Saturday Finally Comes

It was a beautiful August day, a perfect day for the opening game. As Amanda stood at the mouth of the players entrance of the newly re-built New Blundell Park Stadium, she couldn't help but bask in the atmosphere. Over 50,000 football fans were in the stadium for the Grimsby Town v Scunthorpe United game, the inaugural game of the New Premier League season.

Up in the visitor's Directors' Box she could see Spud, now the chairman of Scunthorpe United, and his wife, Anna. By the look of Anna, an addition to the family wasn't too far away. In the guest seats she could see Billy and his new wife, Molly. Billy was now the chairman of Rotherham United and the owner of a chain of pubs. Besides Billy was Trevor and his fiancé, Jenner. They had just returned from a three-week holiday in North Korea where they had been presented with twenty-six volumes of speeches made by the North Korean leader when he was three-years-old. Trevor was also the new chairman of Doncaster Rovers.

As she surveyed the crowd Amanda thought back over the last seven months. The initial shock of being told that she was Lord Milford's daughter. The wealth that was now all hers. The gratification in financially helping her mates and many charities, hospitals and old people's homes. The phone call from the new prime minister, Peter Corbett, asking her to become the President of the New Premier League. The fun nights in her new castle in Buckinghamshire deciding, with Spud, Billy and Trevor, which teams would be in the sixteen to make up the league, and the financial help given to resurrect a number of football clubs. There had been great excitement in selecting and helping Accrington Stanley, Bristol Rovers, Barrow, Carlisle United, Charlton Athletic, Crewe Alexandria, Exeter City, Forest Green Rovers, Gillingham, Morecambe, Newport County and Walsall to join their own clubs; Doncaster Rovers, Grimsby Town, Rotherham United and Scunthorpe United in the New Premier League. It had been an invigorating seven months.

Despite that, something was missing. Her mates had all found that missing ingredient; love. Because she was now mega-rich there had been marriage proposals by the score. Several had come from Hollywood celebrities such as Pitt Bradworth, Matt Rugg, Wayne "The Plastic" Dwayne, and Hank Thomson. Even her former boyfriend Jed had called from Thailand where he was a diving instructor. There had even been a proposal from old Ted, the landlord at the Royal Oak. But nothing excited her or stirred her emotions. Despite wealth and fame, Amanda could not find love.

Amanda put these thoughts aside as she looked at the clock in the stadium. It was getting close to three o'clock, kick-off time. Amanda took a deep breath and stepped out onto the pitch in her designer jeans and white, silk blouse. Her long blonde hair was tugged by the slight breeze as she mounted the portable rostrum in the centre of the pitch. The crowd cheered as she was introduced. A microphone was handed to her. Amanda's soft Yorkshire vowels were transmitted through the stadium's loudspeaker network by the ultra-new DDX System, which allowed Amanda to be heard clearly by simply speaking into a hand-held microphone.

Amanda kept it brief. She knew football fans wanted to see football not hear long winded speeches. She talked of the bright future for football in Britain and spoke about her optimism for the New Premier League. She mentioned that Cloud Sports would be the main sponsor of the league and that word-wide television contracts had already been signed. She briefly announced that such big stars as Mickey Messi, Lionel's brother, and Atheisto Ronaldo, Cristiano's brother, were keen to sign for the New Premier League clubs. But she reserved the best news until last. She told the crowd that the 'big six' from the old Premier League had been 'invited' to play in League Two. This news brought a rousing, sustained cheer from the Grimsby and Scunthorpe fans.

Amanda gave a big wave and strode back towards the players' entrance. She turned to give a last wave to the crowd when a young woman approached her and asked if she could take the microphone. Amanda froze and her heart jumped. It was the girl from the now-defunct Anti-Football Police. The one who had interrogated her in the room. The one dressed in black. The one with the beautiful face. The one with the kissable lips.

Her black hair was now longer, but her stunning face was the same and her lips were just as red and pouting as ever. But on this momentous occasion she was dressed differently. The girl was wearing cheap blue jeans, a tight, white T-shirt with a red name tag over her right breast. Tulip, it said.

Amanda stared at her for longer that she should have done. The match officials and the players eased their way

146

around them as they made their way on to the pitch. Amanda recovered enough to grab Tulip by the arm and gently steer her back down the player's tunnel. Tulip went along, willingly.

Amanda steered Tulip into the nearest room, a small cleaner's store room, and closed the door. Jammed up close together, Amanda and Tulip faced each other surrounded by mops and sweeping brushes. Amanda placed the microphone on top of a bucket and gently held Tulip's face in her well-manicured hands.

Out on the pitch, Grimsby Town's captain had won the toss and elected to kick-off. The Mariners lined up in their black and white striped shirts and black shorts, while Scunthorpe United players, in an all-white change kit, held a last-minute player huddle before the players dispersed to their respective positions. With the teams lined up the referee was about to blow his whistle when female voices, punctuated by heavy breathing, could be clearly heard over the loudspeakers thanks to the amazing DDX System. Amanda spoke first.

"I wondered what had happened to you?"

"Nothing happened to me. I do events."

"Soon as I saw you, that day in the interrogation room, I knew."

"Me too."

"I, I wanted to see you again. I missed, you."

"Yeah, I missed you too."

"Your face. Your body. You're beautiful!"

"Yeah, thanks, so are you."

"I, I think I love you. I, I wanted to tell you that. In that interrogation room."

"Me too. I didn't like questioning you. It was just a job. I, I love you, too."

"Oh, yes!"

"Oh, yes, yes!"

The passionate words were followed by a great kissing sound.

The fans laughed good-naturedly at the extra, pre-match entertainment, as the whistle finally sounded and Silvio Battersby, the new Grimsby Town captain, kicked off to start the long anticipated New Premier League era.